MW00613523

Therefore each of you must put off falsehood
and speak truthfully to your neighbor.

—Ephesians 4:25 (niv)

MYSTERIES OF COBBLE HILL FARM

Show Stopper

SHIRLEY RAYE REDMOND

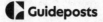

A Gift from Guideposts

Thank you for your purchase! We want to express our gratitude for your support with a special gift just for you.

Dive into *Spirit Lifters*, a complimentary e-book that will fortify your faith, offering solace during challenging moments. Its 31 carefully selected scripture verses will soothe and uplift your soul.

Please use the QR code or go to **guideposts.org/ spiritlifters** to download.

MYSTERIES OF COBBLE HILL FARM

Show Stopper

GLOSSARY OF UK TERMS

Alsatian • German shepherd

backend • autumn

barmy • crazy

biscuit • cookie

brolly • an umbrella

car park • parking lot

chips • fries

cuppa • cup of tea

curd cheese • cottage cheese

daft • crazy, nutty

Guy Fawkes Day • observed on November 5 each year with bonfires and fireworks

Horlicks • malted milk powder

jumper • a pullover sweater

lorry • truck

nick • prison, jail, or police station

peckish • hungry

petrol • gasoline

put paid to • to finish or destroy something

telly • television

torch • flashlight

wellies • Wellington boots

CHAPTER ONE

"Lord Peter Wimsey is fit as a fiddle." Harriet Bailey made the happy pronouncement as she rubbed her hands along the back of a well-groomed Scottish terrier. His coat was black and wiry, his dark eyes twinkling, his nose cold and wet. When she gave him a scratch behind his left ear, the little terrier leaned into her hand, wagging his tail as if to thank her.

Harriet went on. "I'm sure he'll perform well at the dog show. It wouldn't surprise me one bit if he wins Best in Show."

The dog's owner, a short, fiftysomething woman named Gwen Higginbottom, beamed her thanks, her cheeks pink with pleasure. She had dark hair generously streaked with gray. Her blue sweater—or "jumper," as they called it here—made her blue eyes appear particularly bright. "Do you really think so? You're not just saying that to be kind?"

"I really think so," Harriet assured her.

"Petey is a handsome lad, if I do say so myself," Gwen agreed. With a dry chuckle, she added, "He's got a mind of his own, and he's cheeky too, but he's the best dog I've ever owned. Took to the show ring like a pro, even when he was a pup. I was so proud when he won Best in Breed at the regional competition that I nearly burst my buttons." She regarded her pet fondly. "You're the apple of my eye, aren't you, Petey dear?"

Lord Peter, fondly called Petey by those who knew him best, seemed to preen under the attention. Harriet felt certain the dog understood that he was being praised. As she lifted him down from the examination table, she could easily see why he had won competitions in Yorkshire and beyond. Solid and compact with erect ears, a perky tail, and piercing black eyes, the Scottie was a perfect example of his breed.

"He's a dapper little lad." Harriet tried to employ words she referred to as "Yorkshire-isms." It hadn't been easy to learn the different words and expressions used by her British neighbors. She still made plenty of mistakes.

Fortunately, Polly Thatcher, the vet clinic receptionist, proved to be an able and willing tutor. Harriet was now used to filling her vehicle's tank with petrol instead of gas, and she knew that a biscuit was really a cookie, not something warm and fluffy to smother with chicken and gravy or butter and jam. It took some getting used to after more than thirty years of American terminology, but Harriet felt confident she'd get there. She was already familiar with many of the differences after the summer vacations she'd spent growing up with her grandfather.

Polly came into the room with a dog treat, which she offered to Petey. The Scottie sniffed it with a twitch of his little black nose before gently taking it from her outstretched hand. "Isn't he posh in that plaid collar and matching lead?" Polly asked. "The entire village will be rooting for this little man, won't we now?"

Petey wagged his tail, turning adoring eyes on Polly.

Harriet felt her lips quirk up at the corners. It didn't surprise her that Petey had fallen under Polly's spell. Until Polly had begun to date the local constable, the attractive, spunky young woman had half the single men in White Church Bay dogging her heels—pun intended. The animals that visited the clinic all loved her too, as did their owners. Polly had a way of putting those around her at ease.

"I'll admit I'm more than a little antsy," Gwen said. "My stomach is all in knots when I think about the show. I always get fidgety before a competition, but this is the big one. It's being televised, which makes me even more nervous."

"Of course you're nervous," Polly said. "With everyone watching on the telly. Still, we'll all be so proud when Petey takes the top prize. You can count on it."

Gwen turned anxious eyes to Harriet. "Do you think I should have my hair and makeup done? I want to appear professional during the performance, but not overdone. I have to choose my wardrobe carefully. Whatever I wear must be comfortable, especially my shoes, so I can take Petey through his paces without worrying about twisting my ankle or something."

"That makes sense." Harriet hadn't realized there were so many things to take into consideration while prepping for a dog show. One had to do much more than simply show up with a dog and leash.

"Here's hoping our Petey doesn't flop down in the middle of the ring and demand a tummy rub instead of going through his routine," Polly quipped.

Harriet laughed at the mental image, but Gwen responded with an anxious, "Oh dear."

"Petey's a pro," Harriet reminded her. "You'll do fine, and so will he."

Gwen had never married or raised children. Dogs were her life. For years she'd poured all her attention and affection into her terriers. Harriet knew that Gwen was as proud of Petey as any mother might be of her child.

"Petey's well trained and in good health. There's nothing to be nervous about, Gwen. You'll both give it your best, and everything will work out the way it's supposed to." Harriet patted the woman's shoulder.

"That's right," Polly agreed. "Petey won't embarrass you. He never has before, has he?"

"There's a first time for everything." Gwen's grim reply was followed by a shudder.

A few years ago, Harriet's late grandfather, Dr. Harold Bailey, had painted a picture of Petey as a young pup. It was one of the best animal portraits he'd ever done, in Harriet's opinion. He'd captured the lively personality of the confident little terrier, his joyful, independent spirit reflected in the gleam of his dark eyes. It appeared as if Petey had actually smiled for his portrait.

Harriet had to admit, if only to herself, that Petey was one of her favorite patients. Feeling slightly disloyal at the thought, she glanced about for Maxwell, wondering where the little dachshund had gotten to. Though his back legs had been paralyzed when he had been hit by a car, the office mascot was quite mobile in a wheeled prosthesis Harriet's grandfather had acquired for him.

He was probably near Polly's desk, under the watchful eye of Charlie, the office cat. Charlie had been rescued from a burning dustbin as a kitten, leaving her with patchy muted-calico fur. What she lacked in beauty, she made up for in cleverness and a sweet temperament. She was the latest in a long line of office cats named Charlie regardless of gender, a tradition Old Doc Bailey had insisted gave him one less thing to remember.

Realizing that Gwen was watching her, Harriet added another word of encouragement. "As Polly said, everyone in the village will be cheering for you and Petey."

"You're going to be famous, little Petey," Polly said, ruffling the dog's ears. To Gwen she added, "Will you stay in a grand London hotel? I didn't think they allowed pets in their establishments."

Gwen brushed a loose strand of hair from her face. "The ones catering to the dog show crowd happily do so. They offer special rates and even treats for the dogs."

"You know, Gwen, if Petey wins the grand championship, you may become swamped with requests for stud service," Harriet pointed out. "Are you prepared for that?"

"Certainly." Gwen chuckled. "It's about time this little guy earned his keep."

The sound of a bell over the clinic's front door and a man's gruff voice calling out from the waiting room interrupted their conversation. Polly went to greet the newcomer, and Harriet said to Gwen, "My next patient is here. Do you have any other questions for me?"

"No, but I believe I recognize that voice. It's Rupert Decker, isn't it?"

"Yes, he called earlier this morning to see if I could look at Ivanhoe, his German shepherd."

Gwen held up a forefinger. "We call them Alsatians around here, just so you know."

"Thank you." Now that Gwen mentioned it, Harriet recalled her aunt Jinny mentioning that many British people had refused to call the breed German shepherds since World War I.

Tipping her head toward the outer office, Gwen murmured, "Ivanhoe is a fine dog, but I can't say I like the man all that much. I hired him to build some shelves in my spare room a short time ago, and I must say he did a poor job. He also didn't like it at all when I made him come back to remount them. Besides, he's rude. He said some unkind things that I won't repeat." Gwen lowered her eyes, adding in a small voice, "He actually frightened me at the time. In a way, he still does."

"Has he threatened you in any way?" Harriet asked.

Gwen released a slow breath. "No."

Had she hesitated before replying? Harriet couldn't be sure.

She'd met Rupert Decker once before in the village. He was surly, tall, and lean, with short, grizzled whiskers that gave the impression he'd forgotten to shave for a day or two. He'd freely told her he didn't like vets or doctors, so she'd been quite surprised when he'd called to make an appointment for his dog.

All the same, he was concerned enough about Ivanhoe to have Harriet examine the dog. That was a point in his favor. Harriet couldn't abide people who neglected their animals.

"If you need some carpentry work done around your place, I'd advise you to find someone other than Mr. Decker," Gwen said.

"I'll bear it in mind," Harriet replied. Sensing that Gwen would prefer not to pass the surly carpenter and his dog in the reception area, she suggested that they make their exit through her house, which was attached to the clinic.

The woman's face exhibited relief. "How kind of you. Petey does forget he's a pint-size dog. I wouldn't want him to antagonize an Alsatian."

After Gwen was on her way, Harriet mustered her best smile and greeted the newcomer. "Good afternoon, Mr. Decker. What seems to be the problem with Ivanhoe today?" She held out her hand to the large dog, allowing him to sniff her. Once the dog accepted this familiarity, Harriet gave him a welcoming pat on the head.

"He's limping, that's what. Something wrong with his foot or maybe his leg. Can't tell," Rupert Decker said, rising from the chair. He wore a corduroy jacket and a squashed cap. "He growls whenever I try to see it for myself. Figured I'd bring him in and see what you can do about it. You're the expert, so maybe you can help him without getting yourself chewed up in the process."

Harriet and Polly exchanged a glance. Was it possible the grumpy man was afraid of his own dog?

The sound of a car starting outside attracted Rupert's attention. He scowled out the window. "Is that the old Higginbottom busybody sneaking away?"

Harriet ignored the remark and asked him to bring Ivanhoe into an exam room. She watched the dog's gait, recognizing immediately that something was wrong with his front left paw. Perhaps he had a splinter. "Would you like to return to the reception area, Mr. Decker, and have a seat? Polly and I can handle Ivanhoe."

"You think so? He's a big dog, not like that squirt of Higginbottom's."

Harriet resisted the urge to roll her eyes. She'd cared for horses, cows, donkeys, and even llamas. A dog was hardly going to be a problem, even a larger one like an Alsatian. She kept her tone even. "We'll get along fine, won't we, Ivanhoe?"

"I'll stay and watch all the same," Rupert said.

"Suit yourself," Harriet replied as Polly handed her a muzzle of the appropriate size. Ivanhoe had given no indication that he might bite, but any dog could nip when injured, and she didn't know this one yet. The muzzle was a precaution to keep both of them safe.

Harriet made a few other necessary preparations and then rolled a stool in front of the dog. After donning a pair of disposable gloves, she sat down and examined her patient, talking to him in quiet, soothing tones. With disinfectant, sterilized tweezers, and a skill born of considerable experience, she removed a large thorn from Ivanhoe's paw pad, praising him for his bravery. Then she wrapped a stretchy blue bandage around his foot. It wouldn't stay on long, but it would protect the wound for a little while.

"There, all done." She patted the dog's head and flashed Rupert a smile as she removed the muzzle.

When Polly offered the dog a treat, Rupert snorted and muttered something under his breath. The man then mumbled his thanks in a rather reluctant manner.

Harriet replied with a crisp, "You're welcome."

When he followed Polly into the outer office to pay the bill, Harriet tidied the exam rooms and listened to Rupert leave the clinic. She thought again about Petey and realized she resented the man for calling Petey a squirt. The terrier was a bona fide champion. Even if he didn't win the big dog show in London, he had won other competitions. And his charm would always make him a champion in her book.

Harriet had opened a cabinet to check on her supply of disinfectant wipes and alcohol swabs when Polly poked her head into the room. "Van is here. In his official capacity, I might add. He says he has a new mystery for you."

CHAPTER TWO

"Good afternoon, Detective Constable. What can I do for you today?" Harriet greeted Van Worthington with a bright smile as she shoved her hands into the front pockets of her white medical coat. "Is anything wrong? Polly said you needed my help with something."

Van darted a glance in Polly's direction, and his fair skin flushed. He gave the pretty receptionist a shy smile before returning his attention to Harriet. "Hello, Doc. It may be something important, to tell the truth."

Harriet liked the young man. He'd had an obvious crush on Polly for ages. For a long time, Polly had given him no encouragement at all. But recently, they'd begun seeing each other on a regular basis, and Harriet frequently wondered if their relationship might lead to something more serious. It had certainly been a change for Polly, whose social calendar had once made Harriet slightly dizzy.

"I found these in the community lost and found at the station," Van said. "Thought you might know who they belong to. Perhaps you could return them to the rightful owner." He held out a worn dog collar with a name tag attached, along with what appeared to be a medal of some sort. The worn medal was attached to the frayed remnants of a ribbon with broad gray, green, and red stripes.

Taking them from him, Harriet examined the collar and medal. "These appear to be quite old." She fingered the leather collar, which was faded, brittle, and cracked. The small tag had the letters *RIP* on the front. The name of the dog perhaps? The letters embossed on the medal were worn with age and caked with dirt. They were quite difficult to read. The word *Gallantry* in the middle, however, was clear enough. "Where did this come from? I mean, who put them in the lost and found?"

Van shrugged. "Couldn't say. They weren't there yesterday evening when I locked up the station."

Polly stepped closer and gave the collar a casual glance. "I'm taking Maxwell for a walk, and then I'm off for the day."

The little dachshund, hearing the word *walk* and understanding it all too well, scurried to the door, his wheels rolling with a slight squeaking sound.

Harriet chuckled at him. "Thanks, Polly."

Polly slipped on her corduroy jacket and headed out the door with Maxwell.

Van stood watching her retreating figure with a rather wistful expression. Harriet knew the young man was head over heels for Polly, but Harriet wasn't sure if Polly felt the same way, even though she went out with him on a steady basis.

"Help yourself to coffee or tea, if you want some," Harriet said, sitting down at the reception desk. She placed the collar and medal on top to examine them more closely.

"Don't mind if I do." Van made his way to the short counter where the coffee maker was located. "The wind is picking up. It's been blustery all day. Typical backend weather, this is. Wouldn't surprise me if we get a spot of rain too."

Mulling over the term *backend* for autumn, Harriet said, "I don't think these belong to anyone I know. The name Rip doesn't ring a bell either."

Sipping his coffee from a white ceramic mug, Van peered over Harriet's shoulder. "Oh, you think that's a name then? Rip? I thought it meant 'rest in peace.'" He gave her a rueful smile.

Harriet's lips twitched as she suppressed a grin. "I'm pretty sure it's the name of the dog who once wore this collar," she told him. "Right off the top of my head, I can't think of anyone with a pet named Rip. Maybe the dog was seen by my grandfather. I'll check his files."

"I'd appreciate that."

She ran a tentative finger over the collar and then over the face of the medal. "You know, I think these are actually older than my grandfather's day. And I have a feeling they were buried in the ground at one time too. See here? There's dirt caked in the cracks of the leather and around the lettering on this medal."

"That's odd," Van observed. "Who buries a medal with a dog collar? I *think* it's a medal anyway. A war medal maybe. Reminds me of the one my great-granddad received during World War II."

Harriet silently agreed. It did indeed resemble a war medal. But dogs didn't receive medals for gallantry, did they? Her thoughts strayed momentarily to Petey and the many trophies he'd accumulated so far as a champion show dog. But this appeared to be something different.

Harriet rose from the desk and retrieved a bottle of rubbing alcohol and a cotton swab. She gently rubbed the surface of the medal so she could see the embossed letters more clearly. Peering closely, she read them aloud. "'P-D-S-A.'"

"What does that stand for?" Van asked.

"No clue," Harriet admitted. "But now I can make out some more words in the inscription. 'We also serve.'" Intrigued, she glanced up at the constable. "Do you mind if I keep this and the collar for a while so I can do some research?"

Van drained his mug and returned it to the counter. "Be my guest. If anyone comes by the station for those, which I doubt very much, I'll refer them to you."

"That's fine." Harriet felt more than a little curious about the artifacts. "I want to do a little research and see what I can discover." A swarm of questions darted about in her mind. Who had these items once belonged to? Where had they been found? And who, having found them, had left them in the lost and found at the police station?

"Brilliant." Van straightened his shoulders, obviously pleased to be rid of the responsibility. "I'll leave them with you. But I think that must surely be some soldier's war medal. I mean, 'gallantry' is a bit of a tip-off, isn't it? It sounds like something given out during wartime to me."

"Did they give war medals to dogs here in Britain back in the day?" Having not grown up in Great Britain, Harriet wasn't yet familiar with the customs, history, and traditions of the country. She only guessed that a special honor such as this might have been bestowed upon a sentry dog or one who had participated in search and rescue efforts.

"I couldn't rightly say," Van said. "But now that you mention it, I do recall something from my school days about war dogs."

"I'll do a little research and get back to you," Harriet promised. Perhaps she was on the wrong track altogether. Maybe the collar belonged to a dog named Rip and the medal to whoever had owned the dog. She didn't know, but she intended to find out.

Harriet loved the idea that a dog—or any animal, for that matter—might be honored in such a way. Not all heroes were two-legged ones. She knew for a fact that many of God's creatures showed remarkable courage in the face of danger. When instinct told them to flee, animal heroes often exhibited amazing bravery in their efforts to save those they cared for. How often had she read about dogs rescuing people from drowning and cats alerting their owners to house fires? She'd even read about a brave mare that had come to the aid of two children attacked by a wild boar.

"I'll leave you to it." Van straightened his uniform hat. He peered out the window, perhaps hoping to catch a glimpse of Polly and Maxwell returning to the clinic. "You'll keep me informed, won't you?"

"Absolutely."

When he reached the door, Van paused. "One more thing, Doc. I believe I passed Rupert Decker on the road on my way in. Was he here with his dog?"

"Yes. Ivanhoe had a thorn in his paw. I removed it, and he should be fine."

Van pushed his hat back from his forehead. "That surprises me. Rupert isn't one who approves of new faces. I'm surprised he came to see you. When you first moved to the village to take over your granddad's practice, he was quite vocal about his thoughts on 'for-eigners.' He doesn't approve of physicians in general either. He's made no bones about that."

Harriet knew he was referring to her aunt Jinny Garrett, a family physician who lived in the dower cottage next door to the veterinary clinic.

"The poor dog must have been in a lot of pain for Decker to have brought him here," Van said.

"Not anymore," Harriet assured him. "Perhaps now Mr. Decker will change his opinion of me, at least."

Van remained dubious. "Maybe, but he's a rough character. I can't say I trust him. I'd encourage you to be cautious in your dealings with him. Although he has a teenage son, and they seem to get along well."

Harriet recalled Gwen's earlier words of warning about Rupert Decker. "He has a son?"

"Yes. His name is Clarence. He's quiet and not very sociable. The truant officer is well acquainted with him. But in the plus column, Clarence rescues every stray that crosses his path. He seems to prefer animals to people."

Harriet chuckled. "I totally understand that. I like animals more than many people I've met too." She sobered. "Mr. Decker isn't very popular, is he? The town bully, perhaps?"

Van arched an eyebrow. "Not that I'm aware of. No reports of it anyway. I suppose old Decker keeps his fists to himself. Haven't heard otherwise, and in a small village like this one, word would get out."

Harriet gave a relieved sigh. "Good to know."

"All the same, you watch out for Rupert Decker." A chilly gust of wind blew in through the door as Van left.

"Thanks for the warning," Harriet muttered with a shiver. Somehow, she didn't think it was completely from the cold air.

London
November 1940

Dear Malcolm,

Never thought your younger cousin would make it into uniform, now did you? Not with me missing fingers, which disqualifies me from military service. But I'm wearing a uniform now all the same, the official ARP blue serge of a full-time air raid warden. That stands for Air Raid Precautions. I've been fitted out with wellies, steel helmet, armband—the works. I'm finally doing my bit. But I can tell you, conditions in this city are dreadful. Nightly bombings have made them so.

Wardens are supposed to protect people during the air raids. We hand out gas masks and the like and lead folks down into the public shelters as fast as we can. When I started out, I was assigned for three nights a week, but now it's pretty much every night. The Germans think they'll wear us out with this so-called "blitz." They may be right about that—if they don't kill us all off first.

We've got women in the ranks of the ARP too, and they work as hard as the blokes. I guess we've all got to pull together, or Hitler will wear us down to nothing.

When I'm not digging through the rubble searching for survivors, I spend my time ordering folks to comply with the blackout regulations. I reckon you all are doing the same back home, such as keeping windows covered at night so as not to attract the Luftwaffe pilots. Lots of folks here hang blackout curtains. Those that can't afford them use plywood or black paint even.

Have you heard about the Anderson shelters? They're like little metal sheds half buried in the ground in people's back gardens. There's one called the Morrison too, which resembles a metal cage. These are used inside the house. Families all squash in together so they can sleep, and if a bomb flattens their house, they'll be safe inside the cage. At least that's the idea. Still, many people feel safer in the underground stations. When the siren goes off, I start herding people in that direction. It's like leading sheep, which you would know all about, eh?

We wardens are often the first ones out and about after a raid. I make sure folks are safe and try to rescue others from the rubble. I've learned how to give first-aid assistance to the injured, and I spend quite a bit of time fighting fires with water, sand, or whatever is at hand until the fire brigade arrives.

There are six of us in my sector. The other men are locals, and they're happy to have me along. My missing fingers are of no consequence in this sort of duty. We have to be careful, of course. The job has its risks to be sure, such as shrapnel from bombs, falling masonry, and the like. When we started, we had to take down names to learn who resides in our sector. One woman accused me of being nosy and didn't want to give me her name or particulars. But how else can we know who is missing after the bombings?

You said in your letter to me last month that Penny wants to know if I'm homesick. Of course I am. I miss my friends and family. I miss the sights and sounds of home. I miss eating fish and chips on the cliff overlooking the bay.

When we were lads together, we spent hours watching the sea. Do you remember? There's something about the way the colors change and how the sky and water seem to touch at times. Remember how we used to imagine what lay beyond the horizon? We'd make up tales about exotic lands and the different types of people living there, like their customs and the sort of food they ate.

I never imagined at the time that I'd be in London one day, besieged by the enemy, picking through rubble, putting out fires and the like. We must dig out survivors at night, in the dark. Sometimes we can use a torch or a match, but not often because we never know when a pilot will see it and bomb the target again.

You should see the giant puddles in the streets after the rain fills the craters left by the bombs. The roaring from the skies never seems to quit. Earsplitting explosions. The sound of another building collapsing. The smell of smoke and exploded munitions. There's no such thing as a good night here. Your dad said the Great War back in 1916 was supposed to end all wars, didn't he?

Much as I miss him, I'm glad he didn't live to see this. It would have taken the heart right out of him, to learn that such cruelty still exists in the world.

You wouldn't believe the number of animals left homeless by the bombing too. People don't think much about how animals suffer during a war. It's pitiful. The poor creatures are terrified by all the noise and the smoke, and it must be so much worse for them, since they can't understand what is happening or why. Old Blue used to quiver on Guy Fawkes Night with all the firecrackers and such, but this is far worse. We've got strays everywhere—dogs, cats, horses, even birds. When a house takes a direct hit, sometimes all the family is killed except the pets, and where do they go? Fortunately, a local charity has set up about a hundred clinics for injured and homeless animals. They've got their hands full.

And speaking of animals, I've got a new mate. A scruffy little mongrel followed me back to the station the other night after I did my rounds. Poor thing was starving and terrified. I tossed him half my sandwich, and he gobbled it up. Now he follows me everywhere. Friendly little chap. He appears to be smiling half the time, a happy-go-lucky creature despite all he's been through. I call him Rip.

Please thank Penny for remembering me in her prayers. I'm obliged. Thank the good Lord for keeping His eye on me until such time as I can come home.

Your cousin,

Brad

CHAPTER THREE

Later that evening before joining Aunt Jinny for supper, Harriet donned her raincoat and grabbed an umbrella to protect herself from the downpour outside. She was still thinking about the old dog collar, as well as both Gwen's and Van's words of caution regarding Rupert Decker.

As she sloshed along the muddy path that led from her house to the dower cottage behind it, she noted the sunny chrysanthemums in the flower bed near the door. They appeared to glow beneath the porch light, brightening the evening gloom. The dahlias drooped slightly, as if depressed that winter was coming. Harriet loved autumn. She hoped this would be a long one.

She thought again of how much she wanted to succeed in persuading the residents of White Church Bay to accept her as one of their own. She'd made a commitment to do all she could to earn their trust and respect, both professionally as a veterinarian and personally as their neighbor. Aunt Jinny had been a great help in this regard. There wasn't much the woman didn't know about White Church Bay and its residents. After all, folks often confided in their physicians as much as they did their priests and pastors. And Jinny Garrett was the sort of gentle, understanding woman who was easy to confide in.

Harriet heard a car start. Glancing over her shoulder she recognized Alistair Marling exiting the parking lot. Tall with blond hair turning to silver, Alistair was an insurance representative with a one-track mind—sell, sell, sell. He'd been known to pitch policies to people coming down the church steps after Sunday services. Harriet made sure he was out of sight before proceeding to her aunt's door and knocking.

"I see you've had a visitor," Harriet said when Aunt Jinny opened the door. She stepped inside, and her aunt relieved Harriet of her dripping umbrella and rain jacket.

Aunt Jinny was fresh and fashionable in a cobalt-blue sweater and slim-fitting jeans. She had a yellow dish towel dotted with daisies slung over one shoulder.

"You mean Alistair Marling?" Aunt Jinny scowled, which was unusual for the good-natured woman. "He won't take no for an answer. He's been trying to sell me a long-term-care policy in case I need to go into a nursing home. He talked to me as though I have one foot in the grave and the other on a banana peel."

Harriet laughed. "I hate to burst his bubble, but you're one of the healthiest people I know."

"Thankfully, he didn't ask to come in. He just dropped off some informational material." Aunt Jinny hung Harriet's jacket on the coat tree. "There's something about that man I don't like," she said. "I can't quite put my finger on it."

"I know what you mean," Harriet said. She could hear a tinge of worry in her aunt's voice. Aunt Jinny was a pleasant person, warmhearted and generous. She didn't enjoy disliking someone and was always willing to give the other person the benefit of the doubt. "Alistair's not exactly abrasive, but he does rub me the wrong way."

"Has he tried to sell you an insurance policy too?" Aunt Jinny asked, ushering Harriet into the cozy, English cottage kitchen.

"Once, when I ran into him before church shortly after I moved here," Harriet replied. "He hasn't stopped by the clinic to speak to me about it. I don't need another life insurance policy. Dad bought one for me after I graduated from college. It's not a large one, but since I have no dependents, I don't need anything more than what I've got. And I already have insurance for my practice."

"Even if you do decide to increase your coverage, don't go through Alistair Marling," Aunt Jinny cautioned. "I don't trust that man. He's so pushy."

Harriet agreed, dropping wearily into one of the wooden chairs with chintz cushions at the kitchen table. "Something smells wonderful." She noticed a basket of muffins on the table, along with a dish of butter. When Aunt Jinny retrieved a shepherd's pie from the oven and placed it in the center of the table, the aroma made Harriet's stomach growl.

"I heard that." Her aunt chuckled. "Shall I say grace?" Aunt Jinny reached for Harriet's hand.

Aunt Jinny was a good cook and loved to bake. She frequently had her son, Anthony, and his family over for a meal, especially on Sundays. But tonight, it was just the two of them, and Harriet liked her aunt's company all to herself. For the next hour, they enjoyed delicious food and lively conversation. The creamy mashed potatoes had been browned to perfection and covered the lamb and vegetables like a snowy blanket. Harriet hadn't eaten much lamb before moving to

England. Her mother in Connecticut made a similar dish using ground beef. But lamb was a common staple here, and Harriet liked it.

She loved her aunt a great deal and couldn't imagine how she'd have managed to settle into her new digs without Aunt Jinny's love and support—and her tasty meals. "You amaze me, Aunt Jinny. You see patients all day and prepare delicious meals in the evening. How do you do it?"

Aunt Jinny chuckled. "I love eating. That's very motivational."

"I love eating too," Harriet said, "but somehow I never seem as motivated as you to prepare real meals."

"More iced tea?" Aunt Jinny asked.

Harriet held up her glass. "My guilty American pleasure." Hot tea was lovely and soothing, but there was something invigorating about iced tea, even on a chilly evening like this one. Polly and the other locals didn't understand its appeal, but for Harriet, iced tea was a happy reminder of her home in the United States.

"Speaking of men who behave oddly, guess who brought his dog to the clinic today with a hurt paw?"

Aunt Jinny tipped her head to one side. "That doesn't narrow down the options nearly enough for me to begin to guess. You'll have to tell me."

"Rupert Decker. He's a bit of a grouch, isn't he?"

"That's putting it mildly," her aunt replied. "I once heard someone say that Rupert's scowl could curdle milk."

Harriet wrinkled her nose. "I believe it. Van told me that Mr. Decker does not approve of veterinarians or physicians."

Aunt Jinny shrugged. "And I don't approve of bullies. I've heard nothing but negative comments about that man."

"Makes me feel sorry for Mrs. Decker," Harriet mused.

"There is no Mrs. Decker," her aunt informed her. "Not any longer. The poor woman died several years ago of cancer. I never met her, as she was being seen by a specialist in Leeds, but I understand she was a long-suffering soul."

Harriet frowned. "Must have been hard to live with the town grouch."

"I really don't know much about him," Aunt Jinny replied. "I don't think anyone knows Rupert Decker well. He's rather antisocial, and Mrs. Decker was shy. Perhaps he's still grieving her in his own way."

"How old is the son, Clarence?" Harriet took a sip of iced tea.

"He's about fourteen or fifteen by now." Aunt Jinny reached for another muffin. "Frankly, I'm surprised Rupert brought his dog to your clinic. As you said, he's been quite vocal about his disapproval of our respective professions. I suppose that might have something to do with the loss of his wife."

"Van was also surprised he came into the clinic," Harriet said. "But there must be some good in the man. He seems to really love his dog at least. Ivanhoe was clearly well cared for, and he behaved himself while I removed that thorn."

"I'm glad to hear it, but you be careful around that man."

Harriet put down her fork. "First you warn me about Alistair Marling, and now Rupert Decker. Are you intentionally trying to worry me?"

"Not at all, but I don't want you to have your feelings hurt if Rupert bites your head off. He can be so rude."

Harriet slathered butter on another applesauce muffin, mulling over her aunt's words. Three times in one day she'd been warned about Rupert Decker's unsavory reputation—first Gwen, then Van, and now her aunt. Harriet hoped she wasn't being naive to think that his reason to come to the clinic was that he didn't want his pet to suffer. Perhaps he'd had another reason. Curiosity, maybe? Or possibly loneliness? It couldn't be easy raising a teenager on his own.

Picking up her fork again, she scooped up another bite of meat and potatoes. She decided it was time to change the subject. "Aunt Jinny, how would you like to help me solve a mystery?"

"Another one?" Her aunt chuckled. "Okay, spill the beans."

Harriet went in search of her bag and returned with the dog collar and frayed medal. "What do you make of these?"

Aunt Jinny examined them closely. "They appear quite old to me. Before my time, certainly. Where did they come from?"

"Van brought them by. He thought I might know who they belong to, but I don't. The name of the dog is apparently Rip." Harriet pointed to the small metal tag attached to the brittle collar.

"Where did Van get them?"

"He discovered them this morning in the community lost and found."

Aunt Jinny slowly rotated the pieces in her hands. "The collar must be quite old. I doubt it belongs to any of your current patients. But it might go back to your grandfather's day. You'd have to check his old files for a dog named Rip. But keep in mind your granddad was born in 1948, so if this collar and medal are from the World War II era or earlier, he wouldn't have been born yet."

"Which might leave me at a dead end," Harriet said glumly.

"You could check with Rand Cromwell too," Aunt Jinny suggested. "He might know something about them."

The town dogcatcher was a man with a gruff exterior but a heart of gold. He couldn't bear to see any creature in need, and he had a special fondness for dogs. Rand was one of Petey's biggest fans.

"I toyed with the idea of taking the collar over to the Pet Pangaea to see if Tamzin remembers selling it to anyone," Harriet said. "But the more I examined it, the more I'm convinced that it's decades old."

"Yes, this collar is much too old for Tamzin Pickers to have sold it," Aunt Jinny agreed. "The leather is so brittle and cracked. And the medallion is old too. Looks like a war medal awarded for gallantry."

"But is it a medal for a soldier or a dog? Have the British ever given medals to war dogs?" Harriet asked.

"I don't know for sure, but it wouldn't surprise me. Folks here are awfully fond of their dogs. Probably as many dogs as humans in our town. It looks to me like these items were buried at one time. See?" Aunt Jinny indicated the dirt caked into the cracked leather.

"That's what I thought too," Harriet said. "And that makes it even more puzzling. Do you think someone buried these decades ago and then recently dug them up again?"

"You're assuming the person who buried them is the same one who dug them up," Aunt Jinny pointed out. "With a little bit of sleuthing, we might be able to figure all of this out. Of course, if these items date back to World War II, it won't be easy. That was more than eighty years ago, and the further in the past we go, the harder it'll be to find records for something as specific as this."

"Let's start with PDSA. Any idea what that stands for?" Harriet indicated the letters with her index finger.

"Not a clue." Aunt Jinny rose from her chair to retrieve her cell phone from the kitchen counter and tapped away at the screen. "Found it," she said after a few moments.

"And?" Harriet prompted.

"The People's Dispensary for Sick Animals. It's a charity." Aunt Jinny scanned her phone's screen. "Apparently the organization has been around for more than a hundred years. They sponsor forty-eight pet hospitals and care for thousands of sick and injured pets every day, especially for pet owners who can't afford the full cost of veterinary treatment."

"Sounds like an organization worth supporting," Harriet said.

"They have teams who visit schools and communities to raise awareness and educate the public about issues that affect the UK's pet population. It appears they are also a leading authority on pet health."

"Wow. I'll have to research them more." Perhaps she could serve as a volunteer or support the PDSA financially. She firmly believed that all animals deserved to live a safe and healthy life. "Does it say anything about this group awarding medals, either to dogs or soldiers or other pet owners?"

"Not that I see here."

"Maybe they'll be able to tell me if I get in touch with them." Harriet felt a need to reunite the artifacts with their owner, or at least a relative. A distant rumble of thunder attracted her attention. "I think I'd better get home before it starts raining even harder. Maxwell will need to go out again, and poor Charlie may already be hiding under the bed. She hates thunder and lightning. But I can help clean up first."

"Poor kitty," Aunt Jinny said sympathetically. "I can handle the cleanup myself. You get home to your pets." She slid the remaining muffins into a plastic bag. Accompanying Harriet to the door, she reminded her, "Don't forget your brolly."

Harriet obediently grabbed her umbrella and the muffins and then hugged her aunt before dashing out, splashing through puddles on her way back to her house. Maxwell met her at the door, barking as if to scold her for being out in the rain. He toddled outside to do his business and then waited for Harriet to wipe him dry with a bath towel and remove his prothesis before settling into his bed. Charlie was nowhere in sight. She would no doubt remain hidden until the weather cleared.

Harriet had just put on her pink flannel pajamas and pulled back the coverlet on her bed when her cell phone rang. Glancing at the rain streaming down the windowpane, she fervently hoped it wasn't an animal emergency in this weather. But at this hour, what else could it be?

She glanced at the screen before answering the call. "Hey, Gwen. Is everything okay?"

"Petey's gone!" Gwen shrieked. "I've searched everywhere and can't find him. Oh, Harriet, he's gone!"

CHAPTER FOUR

Calm down, Gwen, and tell me what happened," Harriet said, trying to keep the alarm out of her own voice.

"Petey's gone. I went to choir practice, and when I came home, he was gone." Gwen choked back a sob.

Harriet glanced outside at the rain, which had slowed to a steady drizzle. Petey must be drenched. Even if he had gone on a walkabout, he'd likely seek shelter at home soon.

"I'm sure the little guy is hiding out somewhere. He's smart. As soon as this rain lets up, he'll come trotting home, you'll see. Someone may even have taken him in out of the rain," Harriet said. She didn't want to go out again tonight unless it was an absolute emergency. And surely this wasn't. Was it?

"You think he's all right?" Gwen asked. "I've driven all through the village hoping to catch a glimpse of him, but he doesn't seem to be anywhere around. And it's still raining, so it's difficult to see anything. He must have slipped out the dog door into the garden. Then he must have wriggled through the gate and made his escape."

"Petey has done this before, hasn't he?" Harriet asked. "Gotten out through the garden gate?"

Gwen's garden was a small patch of grass bordered by petunia beds. Perhaps Petey longed for greener—and larger—pastures.

But on a rainy night like this? Was it likely he'd run away in the rain?

"Yes, my naughty boy has run away before," Gwen acknowledged. "But he was a pup then and smaller than he is now. It would be harder for him to escape underneath the gate."

"Where there's a will there's a way," Harriet quipped.

Gwen's voice dropped to a near whisper. "Do you think someone could have taken him?"

Harriet heard the fear in the woman's tone and hurried to soothe her. "With the soil being soft from the rain, it would have been fairly easy for the little rascal to dig his way underneath the gate. Really, Gwen, I'm sure there's nothing to worry about. He'll be home soon, probably hungry and quite muddy. He'll need a good bath for sure."

"You don't think he's been kidnapped? I've read about people stealing dogs to be used in those lab experiments over in Leeds," Gwen said.

Harriet smothered a laugh. The rumors about horrific animal experiments conducted at the university in Leeds were part of an urban legend that refused to die. "I hardly think we need to worry about that. Petey will be home before you know it, hungry and wet, with his tail tucked between his legs."

"Do you really think so?"

"Absolutely. But make sure you don't scold him. If you do, he might think he's being reprimanded for coming home, not for escaping in the first place. In fact, make sure you praise him so he knows you're happy to see him."

Harriet wished she felt as certain about Petey's escape as she sounded. Wrestling with her conscience, she admitted to herself that she didn't relish the idea of getting dressed again to go cruising around the village in her grandfather's battered old Land Rover looking for Petey. Especially when Gwen said she'd already done that with nothing to show for it. At the same time, even by Gwen's own admission, this wasn't a one-time occurrence. The most logical explanation was that Petey had escaped the yard all on his own and would be home in a matter of hours.

Then she had an idea. "Why not call Rand Cromwell? He may be out patrolling anyway. He gets paid to round up strays."

Gwen gasped with indignation. "Petey is not a stray!"

"But he has strayed from home tonight," Harriet pointed out. "Give him a call."

In a rather faint voice, Gwen replied after some hesitation, "Rand frightens me a little, but I'll call. For Petey's sake."

Harriet understood. Rand Cromwell had a fierce demeanor and gruff manner. As her grandfather used to say, the man didn't suffer fools gladly. But Rand shared Harriet's love for animals and always went the extra mile to see that those he rounded up were cared for properly until they could be returned to their rightful homes or relocated to a new one.

"I can assure you the man's bark is worse than his bite," Harriet said. "Call him. I wouldn't be a bit surprised if he's already found Petey."

"But if Petey's been kidnapped..." Gwen let her statement trail off, the words lingering between them.

"I'm sure Petey has not been kidnapped. He's just up to his old hijinks. You stay put and let Rand search for him. I'm guessing you'll be reunited before the night is over. In fact, if Rand has already found Petey, he'll have put him in the kennel for the night, especially if he came by your place and tried to return Petey while you were out searching."

"Do you think so?" The woman's tone was hopeful. "I hadn't thought of that. I'll call him right now. Thank you, Harriet. Good night."

She disconnected the call before Harriet could respond. Harriet resolved to touch base with her first thing in the morning.

After putting on her robe, Harriet returned to the kitchen to fix a cup of chamomile tea to quiet her mind before she went to bed. She didn't want to fret about Petey all night. She needed to clear her thoughts. Usually, a chapter or two of one of the Brontë sisters' novels did the trick. She was currently rereading *Wuthering Heights,* which she'd been required to read in high school back in the day.

It seemed an entirely different story now that she lived so close to where the novel had been written. She could easily imagine Cathy and Heathcliff tramping the moors together. She also discovered that Heathcliff was not as attractive now as she'd once thought him to be when she was a romantic-minded teenager. He was an intriguing character, but she wouldn't want to marry him.

Harriet carried her mug upstairs to her bedroom. Charlie appeared with a chirped greeting. "Ready for bed?" Harriet asked her. The cat merely gave her a superior stare as she led the way into the bedroom and jumped up on the bed. "You're a grumpy girl tonight, aren't you?" Harriet stroked Charlie's soft fur. "But I like you all the same."

Between the book, the tea, and Charlie's purring, Harriet was soon lulled to sleep.

The following morning, when Polly arrived, Harriet offered her a cup of hearty English Breakfast tea and one of the applesauce muffins that Aunt Jinny had sent home with her the night before.

Polly accepted eagerly. "Never turn down free food. That's what my great-gran always used to say. She grew up during the war, eating turnip soup and other dreadful things." Polly shuddered. "Jinny's muffins are much easier to stomach than that."

"People do what they have to in troubled times," Harriet agreed.

"And speaking of war," Polly said, "what about those items Van brought by yesterday? I thought the medal might be from World War II. What do you think?"

"I think you could be right."

"Can I see it?" Polly asked. "I only had a quick glance yesterday when Van brought it in."

That was when Harriet realized she'd left the medal and the dog collar at her aunt's house. She clapped a hand to her forehead. "I'll let you see it later, after I get it back from Aunt Jinny. This morning, I'd like to help Gwen Higginbottom search for Petey, if he hasn't been found already. He went wandering last night."

Polly grinned. "Little scamp. Can't believe he'd go out in a rainstorm though. He's smarter than that."

"Do I have anything pressing on this morning's schedule?"

"Mrs. Scroggins has an appointment for her cat this afternoon, and you need to make a house call for Dipsy Doodle."

Harriet chewed her lip. Yes, the Willerton family's enormous potbellied pig needed her hooves trimmed again and a regular checkup. The animal was much too large to haul to the clinic, so Harriet had agreed to go to their home.

"I need to speak with Gwen. If Petey hasn't been found, I'll work with her to decide what to do next. Call me if anyone drops in or if there's an emergency."

"Sure thing," Polly said.

Harriet gave her a hug. "Polly, you're an angel."

"Ah, go on," Polly replied, flapping a hand at her even as she gave a pleased smile.

A call to Gwen revealed that Petey had not been found. The woman was in tears. "I didn't sleep a wink last night thinking of my poor boy out there in the rain. Where could he be?"

"I'm on my way," Harriet promised, though given Petey's history of escaping the yard, she still believed that he'd be home, muddy, miserable, and wiser, anytime now.

The morning air felt crisp, and the sky appeared bluer than usual following last night's deluge. Harriet couldn't help but feel hopeful of finding Petey soon. "And please, Lord, let us find him safe and sound." Harriet had decided to walk, which she enjoyed, and the exercise reinforced her optimism.

The winding streets of White Church Bay were less crowded now than during the summer tourist season. Harriet appreciated the chance to admire the colorful buildings and unique architecture, but she also enjoyed seeing new faces admiring those things about the town she'd come to love. Every season had its perks.

Gwen opened the door the second Harriet knocked, her face a mask of anguish. "Thank you for coming, Dr. Bailey."

Harriet clasped the woman's cold hands between her own. "Gwen, it's going to be all right. I'm certain of it. We'll find Petey soon. He can't have gone far. Did you check with Rand Cromwell? Perhaps he's found Petey already."

Gwen's lower lip trembled. "I've already called him, but no luck. He's out looking again now."

"If anyone can find Petey, Rand can." For the first time, Harriet felt a sour feeling forming in the pit of her stomach. Gwen's worry was beginning to rub off on her.

Gwen took a deep breath as if working up her nerve. "Harriet, I know it's an imposition, but would you…could you…walk with me down the street to hand out these flyers?"

Harriet picked up a flyer from a stack on the end table near the sofa. A photograph of Petey appeared in the center with the words, *Lost Scottish Terrier. Answers to the name of Petey.* Gwen's contact information was listed underneath.

"Do you think I should offer a reward?" Gwen's voice was thick with emotion, but she seemed to be doing her best to keep the British stiff upper lip.

Harriet felt a painful tug at her heartstrings. "Isn't it a bit early for that? He hasn't even been missing for twenty-four hours. I'm sure he'll turn up sometime today. He must be hungry and homesick by now." She didn't even want to consider the possibility that the little terrier might be unable to make it home on his own. "Can I take a look at your garden gate?"

Gwen blinked. "If you wish." She led the way out the back door.

A quick glance told Harriet that, despite the rain the night before, there was no evidence that Petey had dug his way under the gate or made any other obvious exit. "Are you sure the gate was latched last night?"

"Yes, quite certain. I'm careful about that sort of thing."

With an even deeper frown, Harriet wiggled the latch. Was it possible that last night's wind and the lashing rain could have lifted the latch, enabling the terrier to escape? It didn't seem likely. When the two of them went back into the house, Gwen retrieved the flyers and divided the stack between them. "If you could take one side of the street, I'll take the other. Maybe someone has seen Petey."

Harriet agreed, although she felt the flyers were rather unnecessary. Almost everyone in White Church Bay knew Petey. His image had appeared in the local paper several times, announcing his latest dog show ribbons and trophies. Still, she dutifully knocked on every door on her side of the street, dropping off flyers and asking residents to call Gwen Higginbottom if they caught a glimpse of Petey wandering about.

At the corner, she crossed the street and entered the Pet Pangaea, to the tinkling of a little bell over her head. The local pet store sold everything from mealworms and wild birdseed to cricket cages and pet toys.

The owner, Tamzin Pickers, was arranging an assortment of chew sticks on the front counter. "Dr. Bailey, good morning. How can I help you today?"

Tamzin was a tall, angular woman who usually wore slim jeans and knee-high boots. Her hair was gunmetal gray, cut in a stylish bob. There was no sign of her husband, who co-owned the business.

Harriet had never heard Roger Pickers utter more than two words at a time. But he was a kind man, and he and Tamzin seemed to make a good team.

Harriet offered the woman a flyer. "Would you mind pinning this to your bulletin board?" She indicated the one on the wall near the front door. "Petey's gone missing, and Gwen Higginbottom is understandably upset."

"Oh, what a shame! How long has he been missing?" Tamzin took the flyer and walked over to tack it to the board with other announcements regarding dog-walking services and available pet sitters.

"He disappeared last night while Gwen was at choir practice."

"She should contact the detective constable," Tamzin said. "Someone might call the police if they found a missing dog."

"That's a great idea, Tamzin," Harriet said. "I'll tell Gwen to call him right away. Between the detective constable and the dogcatcher, we're bound to find Petey in no time."

Reaching into the pocket of her jacket, Harriet produced a list. "I'd like to purchase these items for the clinic, if you have them in stock," she said, handing Tamzin the list. "I can't take them with me now, as I walked into town, but I can send Polly in later to pick them up, if that's all right."

Tamzin skimmed the list. "Certainly. I believe I have all of these items. I'll put the total on your account."

"Thank you," Harriet replied.

The door opened. Gwen stumbled across the threshold with Miss Jane Birtwhistle on her heels. The two women appeared somewhat breathless and pale. Gwen staggered to the counter and braced herself against it.

Tamzin hurried toward her. "Goodness, you're quite wobbly, Miss Higginbottom." Taking Gwen by the elbow, she led her to a folding chair near the rack of dog leads. "Sit down. Take a deep breath."

Harriet followed them. "Gwen, what's the matter?" Her heart lurched with worry. Had Gwen learned something awful?

Gwen opened her mouth to speak. At first nothing came out. She finally gave a sniffle and begged Jane, "Tell her."

The retired schoolteacher straightened her shoulders. "It's about Petey. He's not really missing—I mean, he's not actually lost. Last night I saw a very tall man carrying a dog out of Gwen's yard. Petey has been kidnapped!"

CHAPTER FIVE

"Who was the man?" Harriet asked.

"I don't know who it was. I couldn't make out his face," Jane replied. "It was so dark, and the rain was heavy. He wore a yellow raincoat with a yellow floppy hat pulled down over his head and yellow wellies. That's all I know." Her tone was apologetic, and her shoulders slumped.

As Harriet recalled, Polly had a similar rain outfit. A long yellow coat, a floppy yellow hat, and even yellow rain boots. Whenever she wore them to the clinic, she reminded Harriet of an oversized rubber duck. But Polly wasn't tall, and why would she snatch Petey from his home?

"You actually saw this man carry Petey away?" Tamzin folded her arms across her chest.

"Yes. He carried him on his hip like this." Jane demonstrated.

"Surely you saw what sort of vehicle he drove?" Harriet probed.

"I didn't. Sorry. He walked around the corner with Petey under one arm and disappeared from my view. I'm afraid I didn't pay as much attention as I should have. He moved so purposefully that I assumed Gwen had asked a friend to see that Petey was all right while she was at choir practice and the friend took him home to make sure he stayed inside and didn't catch a chill from the rain.

Gwen has told me before that he loves splashing in puddles so much that he doesn't always come in when he should. It didn't occur to me that something might be wrong until she came to me this morning."

"I told you," Gwen said, addressing Harriet in a somewhat strangled voice. "I told you Petey had been kidnapped. You didn't believe me. You thought he'd run away. And now someone has him and could be far away by now."

The woman was so pale that Harriet feared she might faint. But before Harriet could say or do anything, Tamzin urged Gwen to bend over and duck her head toward her knees. Her sympathetic manner seemed to break a logjam of tears, and Gwen quietly wept.

"Perhaps the man wasn't kidnapping Petey at all," Tamzin said, patting Gwen's shoulder. "Perhaps he saw him running around in the rain and decided to rescue him before he got hurt in the street by a speeding car or something." She raised an eyebrow at Harriet for support.

Harriet shrugged. Who could say what had happened?

"Then why hasn't he brought Petey home?" Gwen lifted her head and stared at Tamzin—or through her. It was hard to tell.

"Maybe the man doesn't know who Petey belongs to," Harriet suggested. She felt a twinge of concern, not just for Petey but for herself too. Of course, it wasn't her fault that Petey had disappeared, but she still felt a small pang of guilt. After all, she'd assured Gwen last night that the little dog had simply escaped from the garden and would show up soon.

Harriet said, "Maybe Tamzin is right and the man Jane saw was simply rescuing Petey from the rain."

"No, that's not how it was," Jane protested. "Petey didn't wriggle out through the gate into the street. I saw the man open the latch and step into the garden. He picked Petey up and carried him out of the yard. Now that I know Gwen didn't ask him to do that, I know he wasn't rescuing Petey. He was stealing him." She gave an indignant huff as she lifted her chin in a challenging way.

"But who would do such a thing?" Harriet asked.

"And why?" Tamzin added.

"Ransom money." Jane pronounced this with a knowing nod.

Tamzin rolled her eyes. "Ransom? Then he'll be sorely disappointed, won't he? He'll soon find out that Gwen is hardly rich."

Harriet agreed. But what other reason could anyone have for stealing the little terrier? And then another idea sprang to mind. "Maybe it was someone you've competed against in one of the regional dog shows, someone who doesn't want Petey to show up in London to win the championship."

"That's possible," Gwen said, sitting up straighter.

"How unsporting," Tamzin declared.

"But possible," Harriet insisted. "Even likely."

As they mulled over this possibility, Jane said, "That young man who goes to Leeds University—what's his name? Billy something? He has a prizewinning dog, doesn't he? Maybe he's competing in the London dog show too. Maybe he snatched Petey so his own dog would have a better chance at winning."

"Billy Brindle," Tamzin said, her eyes lighting up. "He does own a champion chow. A beautiful, well-trained dog. It won a contest last summer, as I recall. It could easily win Best in Show in London, especially if Petey is out of the running."

When Gwen glared at the words, Harriet nudged Tamzin in the ribs with her elbow.

The shopkeeper hastened to add, "But it would be hard to beat Petey. Very hard indeed."

"And Billy is quite tall and thin," Jane said. "Which fits the description of the man I saw."

"Yes, he is very tall," Gwen agreed.

"Actually, when I saw the man last night, I thought perhaps it was that insurance salesman," Jane mused. "You know the one. He's always trying to talk me into buying more policies. I cross the street when I see him walking my way."

"Why would you think it was Alistair Marling?" Harriet asked. "Did the man who took Petey have white hair?" One could always recognize Alistair in a crowd. His snowy mane was quite distinctive.

"How could I tell under the rain hat the man wore? But there was something familiar about the way he walked down the sidewalk."

"Alistair isn't exactly on my list of favorite people," Harriet admitted. "But I have a hard time imagining him swiping someone's dog for any reason."

"Well," Tamzin began slowly, "rumor has it that Mr. Marling is in financial difficulties."

It always amazed Harriet how everyone in the village seemed to know so much personal information about everyone else. "You think he stole Petey for money? I don't believe it. I can't see him writing a ransom note, can you? Besides, he must surely know that Gwen doesn't have enough money to bail him out of his financial difficulties, whatever they might be."

"Extortion," Tamzin said. "Maybe he thinks Gwen's friends will pitch in and help her buy the dog back."

Harriet refused to believe Alistair was the culprit. "If it ever came out that he'd done such a thing, his business would suffer. He might even have to leave town. He could hardly afford to ruin his reputation or go to prison."

"What if someone paid him to snatch Petey? Someone who wants Petey and Gwen out of the London competition?" Jane suggested.

Gwen choked out a sob. "I don't care who took my little Petey. Or why. I want him back. I'll pay whatever they want. I'll find the money somehow."

As Harriet wrapped her arm around the woman's trembling shoulders, Tamzin said cheerfully, "You go on home and calm yourself, Gwen. Someone may have found him already. Don't worry. He'll be returned soon, and none the worse for wear, I'm guessing. You wait and see."

"You think so?" Gwen asked, hope covering her face.

"I do," Tamzin answered firmly.

"Tamzin suggested we call the detective constable to investigate," Harriet added. "This is worth bringing him in on."

"Good idea," Jane said. She put her hand on Gwen's arm. "In the meantime, you need a strong cup of tea with plenty of sugar."

"Just the ticket," Tamzin agreed.

The front door opened, and a customer came in, giving the cluster of grim-faced women a curious glance. Tamzin excused herself to wait on the newcomer.

Harriet and Jane thanked Tamzin for her help then escorted Gwen home. While Jane made herself useful in Gwen's kitchen, putting on the kettle and rummaging around for a biscuit tin, Harriet called Van Worthington. She quickly filled him in on what had happened the night before.

"I'll come speak with Miss Higginbottom immediately," he promised. "We'll look into the matter right away."

Soon the three women sat at Gwen's small kitchen table, drinking tea and nibbling the coconut sugar cookies Jane had found in a biscuit tin on the counter.

After taking a fortifying sip or two, Gwen sighed. "My poor Petey. I hope he's all right."

Harriet patted her hand without a word. She'd been too hasty the night before in assuring her friend that Petey couldn't have possibly been kidnapped, and yet that was exactly what appeared to have happened.

But why? Harriet knew that occasionally bouts of dognapping happened for various nefarious reasons. Once, back in Connecticut, large dogs throughout the state had gone missing. A ring of thieves had been stealing them to use in dogfighting, a despicable and illegal sport. But she hadn't heard of anything like that taking place in Yorkshire.

The most likely explanation was, as they'd discussed earlier, that someone wanted to keep Petey from competing in the prestigious London dog show. If that was the case, they would have to make haste to recover the dog before the show began in less than two weeks.

Harriet hoped Van could come up with some possible leads. She would put the search for the owner of the collar and medal on the back burner for now. Finding Petey was far more important.

Her cell pinged with a text from Polly. Hoodwink and his owner had arrived for their appointment. SORRY. THEY'RE UNABLE TO RESCHEDULE, Polly texted. CAN YOU COME NOW?

Harriet rose. "I've got to go. Duty calls. Van is on his way. He'll take things from here." Turning to Jane, she added, "Be sure to tell him everything you can remember, even if it doesn't seem important. Describe the man who took Petey as thoroughly as you can. We want the constable to have all possible details so he can resolve the situation."

"I will," Jane assured her.

Touching Gwen's shoulder, Harriet promised to contact her later. She stepped outside, preparing to return to the clinic at a brisk pace.

Van passed her in his police car as she rounded the corner. He stopped the car and leaned out the open window. "Quite a dustup, isn't it? Someone stealing little Petey right before the big show."

"You will take this case seriously, won't you?" Harriet asked him. "Gwen's very upset, as you can imagine, and quite concerned about her dog's safety."

Van pursed his lips. "I will take it seriously, Doc. Of course I will. That's my job."

"It seems possible that someone wants Petey out of the competition. That's a motive for dognapping, isn't it?" Harriet asked.

"Sure enough."

Harriet told him about the dognappings for illegal sporting purposes in the States. "I haven't heard about anything like that here, so I suppose it's unlikely that's what's happened. Besides, you'd think that kind of ring would want to steal an Alsatian or another big dog, not a little Scottie like Petey."

"True." Van opened the door and stepped out of his vehicle. "I can ask around about puppy mills. We get all sorts of police bulletins that might provide a clue as well."

Harriet hadn't thought of a puppy mill. They were dreadful commercial dog-breeding facilities characterized by fast production and poor care. The people who operated such farms cared little for the health of the dogs or the conditions in which the animals were kept.

"When I was in veterinary school, I was part of a team called out to rescue dozens of dogs from such facilities," Harriet said. "It's criminal the way the poor animals were kept. I can't bear to think of Petey being confined in such a place. But Scottie puppies are adorable, and I imagine they're in high demand. That's a reasonable explanation for his being abducted, I suppose, but don't suggest it to Gwen. She's already in a tizzy."

"I won't say anything about that. But there's another motive for this kind of crime." He glanced toward Gwen's home. "I intend to pursue the possibility myself, so I'm not sure I'll mention it to Miss Higginbottom. I don't want to make her worry more than she already is."

Harriet frowned. "What other motive?"

Van peeked over his shoulder as if to make sure no one was listening. "Revenge."

CHAPTER SIX

Revenge?" Harriet stared at him. "You can't possibly mean that."
Van grimaced. "I do."

Harriet glanced at her watch. "Listen, I've got to rush back for an appointment, but will you come by later and tell me what you mean?"

"Sure. And don't you worry, Doc. We'll get to the bottom of this."

"Thanks, Van. That makes me feel a lot better."

On her return to the clinic, Harriet could see the sun sparkling on the water in the bay. She didn't like having troubled thoughts on such a beautiful day, but since most days were beautiful here, it couldn't always be helped.

When she arrived at the clinic, Harriet forced thoughts about Petey to the back of her mind. She needed to get down to business. Professionals were handling Petey's case, and in the meantime every one of Harriet's own patients deserved her best.

She greeted Mrs. Scroggins warmly and assured her that it was normal for a cat of Hoodwink's age to have plaque buildup on his teeth. "I can take care of that this afternoon. It will require him to be anesthetized, but it's a very simple procedure, so I don't foresee any issues with it."

Mrs. Scroggins exhaled in clear relief. "Thanks, Doc. I was worried Winky's teeth were going bad or something."

"I'll check them out after I clean them, but I believe they're quite strong under the plaque. Polly will call you later so you can pick him up when it's all over and done with," Harriet said.

"You remind me a little of your grandfather. Something about your eyes," Mrs. Scroggins said as she slung her purse over her shoulder. She gave Harriet a shy smile. "Your grandfather took care of all my cats."

"How many do you have?" Harriet asked.

"Just one at a time," Mrs. Scroggins replied. "Unlike some people I know. I can't fathom how Miss Birtwhistle handles as many as she does and still maintains such an immaculate house."

Harriet smiled. "Neither can I. She's an impressive lady."

After Mrs. Scroggins left, Harriet whisked Winky into the surgery and went to work with Polly lending an able hand. When they had finished, Harriet gently slipped the cat into a cage to sleep it off. Then she packed her medical bag, making sure she had all the necessary supplies and tools before heading to the Willerton Farm to tend to Dipsy Doodle.

While she was doing that, Polly asked, "How is poor Gwen? Has she found Petey yet?"

"No. We've actually learned that he was dognapped." She filled Polly in on what had taken place earlier that morning.

Polly's eyes widened as she raised her eyebrows in surprise. "Poor Gwen. She must be distraught. Who in the world would steal Petey?"

"We don't know yet," Harriet said, more determined than ever to discover the culprit. She was also determined to do so before the big event in London. Both Gwen and Petey deserved their day in the spotlight.

Van arrived as Harriet was putting on her coat. "I took statements from the women," he told her. "And I've been thinking about what Miss Birtwhistle said about a tall man carrying Petey out through the garden gate. Several men come to mind, including Rupert Decker. He's tall, and he has a grudge against Miss Higginbottom. I think I mentioned that to you yesterday."

"Gwen said something along those lines as well," Harriet said. "She doesn't think much of him, or rather she is displeased with the work she hired him to do. Something about shelves and shoddy workmanship."

"That's what I've heard too. And you know how people talk in a small town. Even the littlest infraction can get blown out of proportion."

"Yes, but what does this have to do with Petey's abduction?" Harriet asked.

"Word of mouth is a powerful thing, and Miss Higginbottom hasn't been shy about giving her opinion of Decker's work," Van said. "I'm sure there are those in town who will go elsewhere for carpentry work because of her. Rupert Decker surely resents this. It's hard enough finding steady, paying work these days without someone tanking his reputation."

Harriet pursed her lips and considered what he'd said. "So you think Rupert Decker stole Petey in retaliation? But what does he want? Surely not ransom money."

"He can prevent Gwen Higginbottom from putting her beloved pooch in the big London show now, can't he? She can't win without a dog. And Rupert along with everyone else in the village knows how much this means to her."

Harriet accepted the truth of this. Everyone in White Church Bay knew about Gwen's "great expectations," as they'd come to call her goal of winning Best in Show at the event. But would Rupert let his resentment drive him to kidnap a dog? She wanted to think he wouldn't, as a dog owner himself. Surely, he wouldn't inflict on someone else a situation that would upset him deeply.

Unless that was his goal, to hurt Gwen in the most poignant way he could think of.

Van continued, interrupting her troubled thoughts. "Rupert would know that on Thursday night, Gwen would be at church for choir practice. He's not a churchgoing man himself, but he knows who goes and who sings in the choir. He could sneak into the garden, coax Petey out through the dog door with a treat, and then carry the little guy off into the night. It was dark and raining heavily. He wouldn't expect to be noticed, much less recognized."

"Do you really think Rupert would carry out a grudge that way?" Harriet asked.

"Who can say? He's been even more prickly since the death of his wife. I suppose we should make allowances. But who knows what someone might do if provoked?"

"I don't think he'd harm Petey," Polly threw in. "He couldn't be that mean."

"I don't think so either," Van added. "And if he tried, his son would stop him. I'm sure of that."

"That's good to know," Harriet said.

"Come to think of it, Clarence may have snatched the dog," Van suggested.

"Whatever for? I thought he liked animals?" Harriet frowned.

"He does, more than he likes people, that's for certain," Van replied. "Perhaps he thinks Petey is being abused or exploited. He might imagine that all the training is cruel and not natural for the wee dog. Maybe he wanted to free Petey of that sort of thing."

"Setting the captive free by dognapping him?" Harriet joked.

"In a manner of speaking." Van raised his eyebrows. "There's no telling about those Deckers. They're an odd pair when all is said and done."

Harriet was still thinking about the Deckers a short while later as she drove the Land Rover to the Willerton farm without stalling even once. Maybe she would master the vehicle, which she had nick-named "the Beast," after all.

She performed the necessary duties on the potbellied pig, cautioning its owner once again about overfeeding the portly animal. "No more jelly doughnuts, Mrs. Willerton," Harriet declared as firmly as she could. "I know you love her and she's cute, but it does her more damage in the long run. If she gets much fatter, I'll have to put her on a strict diet."

After leaving the farm, Harriet decided to visit Doreen Danby before returning to the clinic. Sensible, good-humored, and wise beyond her years, Doreen was a great neighbor and was becoming a dear friend. She'd been one of the first town residents to make Harriet feel welcome in the community, and no one knew the locals better than she did. If anyone could give Harriet advice on the Petey situation, it would be Doreen.

Harriet sent Polly a quick text about her plans then headed down the road to the Danby farm. Despite the sunny day, none of the Danbys' five kids were anywhere in sight. Then Harriet remembered it was Friday, and the kids must still be in school.

She knocked on the door, and Doreen answered, wearing an apron and sporting a smudge of flour on one cheek. A wonderful aroma wafted through the house. Harriet sniffed appreciatively, realizing that she hadn't had lunch yet.

"Why, Harriet, what a pleasant surprise," Doreen said, clearly delighted to see her. She ushered Harriet into the kitchen, made her take a seat at the table, and served her a meat-filled pastry rather like a savory turnover.

"Oh, yum," Harriet said after taking a bite. "This is heavenly." The filling was seasoned wonderfully, surrounded by buttery, flaky pastry.

Doreen bustled around for a cup and saucer for Harriet's tea. "Now, much as I love a casual visit, something makes me think you're here for a specific reason."

"I am. Can I pick your brain about something?"

"Sure." She appraised Harriet's expression and sat down with cups of tea for both of them. "What's troubling you?"

Harriet launched her tale from the beginning, telling her everything about Petey's disappearance and Jane's sighting of the dognapper.

Doreen listened attentively, and when Harriet was done, she sat back in her chair and crossed her arms. "It will be a crying shame if

Gwen and her dog can't participate in the London show. Everyone's been talking about it. My Tom says they're all talking down at the pub about how Petey might win the grand championship. Petey's a local favorite, the little scamp. He's full of sauce, that one."

"Petey will do us all proud," Harriet said. "I'm certain he has a good chance of winning the top prize—if we can find him in time."

"What sort of criminal charges can be brought against a villain who steals a dog?" Doreen wondered out loud.

"I don't know. I'll have to ask Van," Harriet replied. "My main concern now is getting Petey back safely."

"Any possible suspects?"

"Too many," Harriet said. She began listing them.

At the mention of Alistair Marling, Doreen snorted. "He's a nuisance, but I have a hard time imagining him as a dognapper. He wouldn't want to muss his expensive trousers. That man spends more on clothes in one month than I do in a year."

"Billy Brindle's name came up too," Harriet went on. "I haven't met him. I understand he's a university student over in Leeds."

Doreen nodded. "Nice lad. Can't imagine him kidnapping Petey either. And why he would is beyond me. He's got his own blue-ribbon dog. Although I'm guessing he's too busy at university to go to London dog shows."

"What about Rupert Decker?"

At this, Doreen heaved a sigh. "He's a nasty piece of work when his temper is aroused. Tom hired him to do some work around here last year and doesn't intend to do so again. Rupert's too hotheaded and doesn't take orders well. Poor soul. He's never quite gotten over the loss of his wife, I suppose."

"You think him capable of such a thing? Snatching Petey, I mean."

"Nothing he does would surprise me," Doreen said. "But why steal the dog in the first place? Can't sell him anywhere around here. Petey is too well known, so I don't think he'd get any takers. What's the point of taking him?"

"Revenge?" Harriet offered the possibility that Van had proposed. "I understand there's bad blood between Rupert and Gwen. Maybe he took Petey so she can't participate in the London competition."

Doreen mulled that over. "That's a possible motive. I can buy it. It's the sort of unneighborly thing he might do to get even with Gwen. Even though his quality of work is no one's fault but his own."

"So if that's really his motive, do you think he'll return Petey after the London dog show is over and done with?" Harriet asked.

Doreen raised her eyebrows. "It's hard to know what Rupert will do, especially when we don't know his motive. If he even did it."

"I don't think he'd hurt Petey," Harriet ventured to say after more consideration. It was a hunch, but she hoped it would prove true. "He brought his dog Ivanhoe to the clinic yesterday so I could remove a thorn from his paw. The dog appeared to be in good health—well fed and cared for. Rupert Decker can't be all bad, right?"

Doreen smiled. "Rupert brought his dog to your clinic? Will wonders never cease. He's been vocal about his disapproval of medical professionals. I reckon that includes vets."

"Word around town is that it has, but perhaps yesterday was the first step to changing his mind. What about his son, Clarence?" Harriet probed.

Doreen refilled Harriet's teacup and then her own. "The lad seems to be fine, but he's very shy. Goes to school with our Thommy and is about the same age. Clarence is quiet and rather awkward. Some kids bullied him in the past, but he's got a gentle way with animals, and they respect him for that. Thommy likes him well enough, but they aren't really friends. All in all, Clarence keeps to himself."

"And he wouldn't hurt Petey, right?" Harriet went on. "If he took Petey, or if Rupert did, Clarence could be counted on to care for him, right?"

"Sure. The boy has a big heart for animals, and he's good with them too. He'd make a good vet or animal rehabilitator someday. He's always rescuing something. Foxes, birds, even hedgehogs. Thommy said he came to school one day with a baby owl in his coat pocket. Caused quite a stir. He insisted the bird needed frequent care and the best way for him to provide it was to keep it with him."

Harriet glanced at her watch. "It's too late in the day now, but maybe I should go out to the Decker place tomorrow. While I'm there, I can follow up about Ivanhoe and poke around for any signs of Petey."

Doreen reached over to clutch Harriet's hand. "Okay, you do that, but promise me one thing—you won't go out there alone. Take someone with you. If Rupert is in a foul mood—Well, who knows what he might do?"

London
December 1940

Dear Malcolm,

Well, as you can imagine, the continuing air raids have put paid to any chance of a decent night's sleep. My mate Garrick lives with me in the section station. We're both unmarried, so they figure we'll put up with the simple living. For example, the beds are about the size of a shelf in your kitchen pantry. On my off-duty nights, I always plan to hit the sack early and get a good night's sleep after drinking a cup of Horlicks. Then come the bombers. I think they time it just to spite me. No signs of fire this morning when we knocked off, but I did see smoke curling up over the rooftops in another sector.

I'll try to get some shut-eye this afternoon before I go on duty tonight. Want to write you a letter first and get it in the post. Need to wash out my socks and such too. I start most days with a strong brew and a bit of toast with oleomargarine and a scrape of jam or marmalade, if we can get it. We're learning to fill the kettle the night before in case the Luftwaffe hit the water main again.

Speaking of jam, I surely appreciate the plum cake Penny sent and the jar of strawberry jam. Both are fine. Garrick and I had a feast when the package arrived.

I sure hope Penny didn't use up all your sugar ration on me. It's nearly Christmas, and you've got the kids to think about and all.

We shared a bit of plum cake with Rip too. He's become the mascot for our section and follows me about when I make my rounds. Rip seems to know what to do without being told—digging in the rubble, searching for survivors. In my book, he's a real home-front hero, and can he dig!

All too often, we find ourselves dealing with recovery instead of rescue. No need to share that part with the missus. But when we do rescue a dog or cat and can reunite the poor creature with its frantic owner, it's a real morale booster for us all.

I should mention the PDSA—the People's Dispensary for Sick Animals. That's the charity I told you about in my previous letter, the folks that set up clinics for injured and lost pets all over London and beyond. Have you heard of them? We find them setting up shelters everywhere. I'm as fond of animals as a man can be, so I'm thankful they've taken the problem in hand.

You asked if this section of the city is the same as when you visited some years back. No. The roads are usually clogged with fire hoses and cordoned off because of bomb damage. Sandbags are stacked everywhere. You wouldn't recognize the place. Wouldn't recognize me either after a shift. Sometimes our jackets and trousers are covered in plaster dust, our boots scuffed, and our faces streaked with soot. Can't reasonably stay clean after scrambling over scorched wreckage as we try to pull people from under another ruined building.

Just yesterday we went to a house—or what was left of it. An oak wardrobe leaned against the last standing wall. The floor sagged. Ragged stumps of joists were exposed. Piles and piles of bricks, tiles, and timbers. Someone's entire existence had been reduced to nothing.

Rip bounded up the heap of rubble, listening for anyone who might be trapped. We guessed everyone was lost, that there would be no one to rescue. But Rip, he's always sharp. He scrambled up a heap of bricks and barked his head off. Garrick and I followed. Sure enough, he'd located a little boy who couldn't have been much more than four years old, trapped beneath the rubble and safe as could be—no bones broken, no injuries. Good old Rip came through again. Then to top it all off, he found the boy's parents as well, both with minor injuries, but they'll survive.

That same night, we dug out an elderly couple, who were thankful to be alive. Took them to the rest center for a cuppa and a washup. They're going to be all right, and the little lad and his folks will be too.

We have to be mindful when rescuing—go slow, be thorough. We can easily miss someone if we don't search the rubble well enough. Some days we find fewer survivors than we'd like. Those are hard days. Yesterday was sad. Even Rip seemed to feel it.

Garrick was a soldier in the Great War, and he always says he doesn't know what was so great about it. Too many men cut down in their prime. I said I guessed he was used to seeing dead bodies. He told me no one gets used to seeing so many dead.

After rescuing and recovering people, then comes the cleanup. After all those years with you and your dad on the farm, I've got the muscles for lifting and shifting. We generally tidy up the site as much as we're able, trying to make it safe, you know? Prop up the dangerous walls and the like.

The heavy rescue units come in their big Austin three-ton lorry with their shovels, picks and crowbars, ladders, wheelbarrows, ropes, and other tools. Some of them are men too old to be soldiers who still want to do their part, and others are young men, boys really, who feel the same. I'm thinking of getting a lorry license. There's a great need for able truck drivers. No doubt it will be the same once we win this war and can start building up the city again.

Have I mentioned the Salvation Army lasses? We call them the Sallys. They come round with their mobile canteens following a bombing to bring hot tea and currant buns, even fresh doughnuts sometimes. They are tireless volunteers. I'm always right peckish after working the night shift. There's nothing like a good cuppa and a currant bun to help put things right. There's one girl in particular, a pretty one named Susan. She brightens the wee hours with her smile and kind words. When we have time for a chat, the two of us get along like a house on fire. If things were different, I'd ask her to walk out with me.

We keep watch for blackout violations too. Had to write up the greengrocer on charges again this week. He'd left a light on in his store and forgotten to close the blackout curtains. We knocked and knocked at his door, but he wasn't home. Garrick broke the glass in the front door, and we let ourselves in to switch off the light. You wouldn't think it, but even such a small thing is worse than a lighthouse for guiding the bombers to our sector.

I heard they charged him thirty pounds in magistrate court. That's about two months' wages for those of us full-time in the ARP. He got right sniffy about it too. The old bird won't make that mistake again, will he? We must hope not, anyway.

Garrick says paying a fine is too good for such care-lessness. He says the bloke should have to do rooftop spotting for a month to learn the importance of observing the blackout regulations.

I fill out a lot of forms back at our section station. But it's all done and dusted now. Time to get some rest. But I wanted to get a thank-you for the treats in the post first thing. Glad you're not having bombing up there in York. Stay safe and well. And have a happy Christmas despite everything.

Your cousin,

Brad

CHAPTER SEVEN

L ater that evening, Harriet toyed with the idea of driving to town for fish and chips. It was Friday night after all. But she just wanted to relax. Besides, she was tired and not all that hungry, since she'd consumed not one but two of Doreen's tasty meat pies.

Polly had a date with Van. The couple intended to drive to Whitby for a movie, then dinner at a new fusion restaurant. Harriet wasn't quite sure what sort of food Polly had been talking about. Come to think of it, Harriet couldn't remember the last time she'd gone to see a movie. It was so much easier to stay home and watch something on television.

Besides, she was worried about Petey and Gwen, and she didn't really feel like being around people. A bowl of chicken noodle soup might be exactly what the doctor ordered.

Harriet had just changed into her sweats and slippers when her cell phone rang.

It was Aunt Jinny. "Hey, Harriet, I'm on my way to play cards with the girls, but I wanted you to know I discovered something else about the PDSA. They awarded medals of honor called the Dickin Medal to gallant animals during and immediately after World War II. I've emailed you the link if you want to do some research of your own."

There was nothing Harriet could do for Petey or Gwen at the moment, so perhaps it would be nice to get a break from that with a less stressful mystery. "Thanks, Aunt Jinny. That's good to know. I'll check it out. By the way, I accidentally left the collar and medal at your house last night."

"I found them and will drop them off on my way out," her aunt said. "There was a photograph online of the medal with a green, red, and white ribbon attached. It matches the frayed one on the medallion Van gave you."

"I suppose that solves one piece of the puzzle," Harriet mused.

"With a little more research on your part, I'm sure you can discover if a dog named Rip ever received the Dickin Medal. You can probably find out why he received it too."

In that moment, Harriet knew how she intended to spend her Friday evening, and she truly looked forward to it. Digging into the past would make a pleasant distraction from fretting about Petey's whereabouts. She also wanted to call Van to ask if he would accompany her to the Deckers' home in the morning. They would have to come up with a plausible reason for stopping by. Rupert Decker might be gruff and rude, but he wasn't stupid. Harriet had guessed that much. He'd see through any ruse in a minute. Then they'd get nothing out of him—whether information or cooperation.

"If the medal did belong to a local dog and if it dates back to the war," Aunt Jinny continued, "you might even be able to find some information in your great-grandfather's files."

"There aren't a lot of those left," Harriet reminded her. "Grandad purged a lot of his father's records through the years."

"True," her aunt conceded, "but you won't know for sure if you don't check. I'll be over in a bit."

Moments later Aunt Jinny knocked at the door. She was lovely in jeans and a dark green blazer. She'd styled a colorful scarf around her neck to complete her ensemble. Maxwell raced to greet her. After handing the collar and medal to Harriet, Aunt Jinny leaned down to pat the dachshund's head. "Harriet, do you want to come with me? The girls won't mind. There's always room for one more at the card table. It seems a shame for you to stay home alone on a Friday night."

Smiling, Harriet shook her head. Now that she had a lead regarding the Dickin Medal, she was eager to do some digging. "I think I'll pass, but thanks for asking. I really want to learn more about Rip and his medal."

Aunt Jinny peered closely at Harriet's face and frowned. "You're a little pale, dear. Are you coming down with something?"

Harriet laughed. "Do you want to feel my forehead? I'm fine, really. It's been a long day, that's all. I haven't told you about Petey being dognapped, have I?"

"What? You're kidding." Aunt Jinny appeared flabbergasted.

"Unfortunately, I'm not. He was missing when Gwen got home from choir practice last night."

"Are you sure Gwen Higginbottom isn't blowing this all out of proportion? Maybe Petey simply ran away. He's done that before, you know. He'll turn up sooner or later, don't you think?"

"No, there was an actual witness to the dognapping. Jane Birtwhistle saw the whole thing." In a few brief sentences, Harriet provided the rest of the details.

Aunt Jinny frowned. "That's awful. Who would do such a thing? And right before the big show in London too. Gwen must be beside herself with worry."

"She's quite distraught," Harriet said.

"And you say Jane actually saw the man who took the dog?"

"Yes, but not his face," Harriet replied. "We've come up with quite a list of possible suspects. And it might be someone we haven't even thought of."

Her aunt glanced at her watch. "I'm running late. Can we talk about this more tomorrow?"

"Sure, but I'm guessing you'll hear all the details at your card party," Harriet said with a grin. "You know how gossip and news spread through the village like wildfire. Gwen and I distributed flyers up and down her street. Rand Cromwell and Van have been out searching for Petey too. By now nearly everyone in town knows the little Scottie is missing."

"It's a shame. I hope he'll be found soon." Aunt Jinny gave her a hug. "Take care of yourself. Go to bed early. Doctor's orders."

Harriet gave her a mock salute. "Aye-aye, Captain."

After sending her aunt on her way, Harriet placed the collar and medal on the end table in her living room and went in search of her laptop. With a mug of soup, she settled herself on the couch. It was time to do a little investigation into the Dickin Medal. Her aunt's link took her to the PDSA website. From there, Harriet found the information she wanted.

The PDSA Dickin Medal was established during the war in 1943 by an animal lover named Maria Dickin, who had also founded the PDSA. She wanted to honor the noble work of various animals during World War II. The medallion, cast in bronze, bore the words *For Gallantry* and *We Also Serve.* It was attached to a tricolor ribbon identical to the faded, frayed one Van had discovered in the lost and found. The animals deemed worthy of receiving the award had to be associated in some way with the Armed Forces or the various Civil Defense or Civil Emergency units.

Harriet was quite surprised to learn that the medal had been awarded fifty-four times between 1943 and 1949. Recipients included thirty-two pigeons, eighteen dogs, three horses, and even a stray cat that had "served" aboard a British Navy ship. Several of the recipients received full military honors when they died, and were buried in a special cemetery.

Harriet's pulse quickened as she continued to scroll through the list of recipients. Yes, there he was—Rip. She felt a surge of excitement at the discovery. Rip was a mixed-breed terrier who'd served as a search and rescue canine in London during the Blitz. He'd received the medal in 1945 for services rendered.

There was no mention of who had owned the dog.

She continued to dig through the website for more information, but she found nothing else pertinent. Still, she'd found one answer at least. But while the entry answered some questions, it left many others unanswered. Who was Rip's owner? Did he originally hail from White Church Bay, or was he a London native? And how in the world had the dog's collar and Dickin Medal wound up in the lost and found at the local police station?

Harriet chewed her bottom lip, lost in thought. She was moving forward, true, but by inches rather than the leaps and bounds she wished for. Recalling the lost and found at the police station caused her focus to shift to Van Worthington and once again to Gwen's missing dog. If Petey wasn't found in time, he wouldn't be able to win that championship at the big London dog show—an honor Gwen hoped for with all her heart. If Petey happened to be injured in any way from his unfortunate escapade, it might take a while for him to recover, which meant they had even less time to lose.

She glanced at the lower right-hand corner of her laptop. Not too late. And surely Van and Polly had left the movie theater by now. Much as she hated to interrupt them, she had no idea what time the date would be over, and she didn't want to try to contact him too late.

She made the call before she could change her mind. As soon as the young detective constable answered, Harriet blurted out her request. "Van, will you go with me to see Rupert Decker tomorrow morning?"

Without hesitation, he answered, "Certainly. I suppose this has something to do with Gwen Higginbottom's missing dog."

"Yes, it does. I'd like to question Rupert and his son, but I don't want to go there alone," Harriet said.

Van cleared his throat. "No, going alone would not be wise. Not that I think Rupert would harm you, but…" Van left the remainder of his comment unfinished before adding, "Really, you should leave the investigating to the experts."

"I know, but my presence will add plausibility to your reason for being there," Harriet said. "Do you think we need to come up with a cover story?"

"No need to fret about that," Van said, his tone lighter. "The truth is always the best way to go. I'll inform him that I'm making official inquiries into the disappearance of Miss Higginbottom's dog, and you can inquire about how his is recovering after his appointment with you. I am, in fact, calling on as many people as possible, hoping someone might have seen or heard anything relevant to the case."

Harriet felt an immense relief. "He can't possibly take offense at that, right?" She heard the note of eagerness in her tone. Her heart fluttered with excitement. Or was it trepidation? She wasn't particularly eager to meet up with Rupert Decker again. But she looked forward to any answers they might find. Whether Petey was there or not, the visit would help to shape the investigation. "You've been working all day on this, and I'm sure both of us will continue to do so until we get some answers. We can assure Mr. Decker that we're not singling him out."

"Right you are," Van replied. "I can pick you up around ten if that's convenient. It will give me time to stop by the station and take care of a few things first."

"I'll be ready," Harriet promised. "We need to find Petey as soon as possible. The dog show is less than two weeks away."

"I'm doing my best to get to the bottom of this as quickly as possible," Van assured her.

"Thank you, Van. I know you are. See you in the morning."

Harriet placed her phone beside her on the couch. Yes, they needed to make haste. The clock was ticking.

CHAPTER EIGHT

The Decker home proved to be a modest, whitewashed brick house with a slate roof. It was as far from the heart of the village as one could get and still be a part of the community. There were no shrubs or flower beds in sight, except for some dried hollyhock stems leaning wearily across the front of the house. The ungroomed grass grew as it wished. But the cliffside ocean view was breathtaking. Not for the first time, Harriet realized how blessed she was to live in such a lovely place. The Deckers' nearest neighbor was about half a mile away. It was a perfect place to hide a small dog, she noted.

As Van pulled his vehicle to the front of the house, Harriet spotted a goat tethered in the front yard. The animal raised its head at their approach but soon returned to grazing. Harriet caught a glimpse of wire cages and wooden pens to the side and around the corner of the house. That must be where Clarence Decker kept his menagerie of rescued animals. Was he keeping Petey in the back somewhere too?

"It's a rather lonely spot," Harriet observed.

Van responded with a mild snort. "I reckon Rupert Decker likes it that way—far from prying eyes and nosy neighbors." They exchanged a knowing glance.

As they stepped out of the vehicle, Harriet felt an uptick in her pulse and a slight tingle of dread along her spine. She wasn't sure whether she was nervous or excited. Maybe a little of both.

"I think it would be best if I do the talking, considering Decker's low opinion of medical professionals," Van said in an apologetic tone. "Besides, I'm the investigating officer. No offense meant, Doc."

"None taken," Harriet assured him. "I know Rupert is rather intolerant of doctors, and I don't want to irritate him more than necessary. Besides, as you say, you're the detective constable, and we're here on official police business."

"That's right. And you're here in a professional capacity to check on the dog."

Before either could say anything else, the front door opened and Ivanhoe bounded out, barking an alarm. Right behind him was Rupert Decker—lean, scraggly, and unshaven. The tall, loose-limbed man wore baggy denim jeans and a denim shirt, untucked. He held a mug in one hand. The other hand was shoved deep into the front pocket of his jeans.

Van stiffened as the German shepherd dashed toward them.

"Stand still," Harriet cautioned. "Let the dog get used to our presence."

Rupert snapped, "Ivanhoe, meet." The dog stopped and fell silent.

Harriet took a slow step forward, holding out her hand for the dog to sniff. Ivanhoe did so and then slowly wagged his tail. He must remember her and had accepted them as friends.

"What do you want out this way?" Rupert demanded.

"Good morning, Mr. Decker," Van greeted him in a cheerful tone.

Rupert flicked a glance in Harriet's direction. She forced herself to maintain a neutral expression. She didn't want to appear distrustful, although she was. Nor did she want to appear too friendly. That would only serve to raise the man's suspicions.

"I wanted to see how Ivanhoe is doing," she told him.

"He's fine, as you can see." Turning to Van, Rupert repeated, "What are you doing here?"

"Gwen Higginbottom's dog has gone missing," Van said, keeping his tone even and calm. "I've been making inquiries throughout the neighborhood. Have you seen the dog by chance? He's a black Scottish terrier. Answers to the name of Petey."

Rupert harrumphed. "The Higginbottom woman is daft, and so is her dog."

With considerable effort, Harriet held her tongue. Arguing with him would accomplish nothing.

"You're entitled to your opinion," Van said rather sternly, "but I'm required to investigate the animal's disappearance all the same."

"When did it go missing?" Rupert patted his thigh, and Ivanhoe trotted to his side and sat.

"Thursday night," Van answered. "It was dark and raining hard. The dog might be injured or lost."

Harriet noticed that the detective constable had not mentioned that there had been a witness to Petey's abduction. Probably for the best at this point. If Rupert was guilty, they didn't want to tip him off that he'd been seen. He probably wouldn't respond well to such information.

A teenager slowly rounded the corner of the house. Clarence Decker, she presumed. He was tall—even taller than his father in fact. He had a pale face with a messy thatch of dark hair. He wore jeans and a burgundy sweatshirt. Despite the October chill in the air, he was barefoot. In his arms, he cradled a brown rabbit with a splint on one leg.

Harriet eyed the rabbit, unable to resist examining an injured animal. "You've done an excellent job at splinting that leg."

The boy's face remained impassive, but something in the way his posture changed indicated he was pleased by her praise. "You're the lady vet then?"

"I am. My name is Harriet Bailey." She smiled at him, but she didn't offer to shake hands, not wanting to risk him dropping the injured rabbit. She could practically feel Rupert's suspicious glare boring a hole in her back.

"You took the thorn out of Ivanhoe's paw," Clarence went on. "I tried, but I didn't have tweezers, and I was afraid of making the situation worse."

"That was a good call," Harriet told him. "I have extra tweezers. I'll give you a pair. They'll come in handy the next time."

"Oh, thank you." The boy's brown eyes widened. He seemed slightly disarmed by her generosity. "So Petey is still missing?" Harriet stood close enough to him to spot the smattering of freckles across his nose and cheeks. "Someone was passing around a flyer."

Van joined the conversation. "Yes, and we're hoping to find him as soon as possible. The dogcatcher is on the lookout too."

"I'm afraid the poor little guy might be sick or injured," Harriet said. She hoped to play to the boy's natural sympathy for animals.

"The sooner we find him, the sooner I can get him on the road to recovery to make sure he can compete in his big show in London."

Scowling, Rupert moved toward them. "You came out here thinking my boy has that woman's dog." It was an accusation, not a question.

"Not at all. As I told you before, we're making inquiries in the neighborhood," Van assured him. "We've spoken with several others, hoping that someone has seen Petey since he disappeared Thursday night. We'll continue to do so until the case is resolved."

Rupert softened—but barely. He cast a hard glance at his son. "It's true my lad picks up every stray he finds between here and Liverpool." He shook his head. "But he hasn't brought home any pampered poodles of late."

"Scottish terrier," Van corrected him.

While Van described Petey for Clarence, Harriet peered around the corner of the house, trying to get a better look at the animals in the pens and cages. From where she stood, she could make out a pacing fox, a duck with an injured wing, and some sort of hutch that appeared to house another rabbit perhaps. She would have enjoyed a tour of Clarence's little animal clinic, but she decided this was not the best time to ask for one.

"If you're thinking we took that dog, you can think again. We were at the Crow's Nest playing darts that evening." Rupert tilted his chin toward Clarence. "Ask anybody. They'll remember."

"And why's that?" Van asked, frowning slightly.

Rupert grinned, and Harriet wished he'd do that more often. It made him a lot less scary. "Because I won. Took on all comers, I did, and beat 'em all. Ask my son here. Ask anybody." There was no mistaking the challenge in his tone. Or the pride.

"As you haven't seen the dog, we'll be going," Van said, giving Harriet a sharp glance. "We have more people to speak with. If you find the dog wandering about, please call the station immediately."

"We'd appreciate your help in keeping an eye out for Petey," Harriet said to Clarence. "I'm worried about him." Then thrusting her chin toward the pens and cages, she added, "I'd like to come back sometime and see your menagerie."

The boy gave a curt nod as he stroked the rabbit's ears absently.

Neither Van nor Harriet spoke again until they were well away from the house, heading to the village.

"Do you believe him, Doc?" Van asked. "Do you believe they didn't take the dog?"

"It will be easy enough to verify their alibi," Harriet replied. "We know what time Petey was carried off. If Rupert and Clarence were indeed at the pub playing darts during that time, then they couldn't be the culprits."

Van pursed his lips, considering this. "Of course they could have paid someone else to snatch the dog."

"True, but Rupert strikes me as the thrifty type. I doubt he'd pay someone to do something he could easily do himself—no matter how big a grudge he has against Gwen. He wouldn't part with his money for something like that." Harriet peered up at the clear blue sky. "It's too bad it's not raining today."

Van gave her a puzzled frown. "You've got something against a lovely day like this one?"

"I'd liked to have seen what they wear in the rain." Harriet chuckled. "Okay, I have to say it. I can't see either Rupert or Clarence wearing bright yellow rain gear from top to bottom. Both of them would look like giant rubber ducks."

Van laughed. "I pictured it, and I have to agree. Though some people don't really care how they appear to others. All the same, I'll call in at the pub and ask around. But I'm guessing Decker was telling the truth. It would be too easy to catch him out in that particular lie, so there's no point in telling it if it's not true."

"Which pretty much leaves us back where we started," Harriet said, the amusement fading.

Van sobered as well. "Unfortunately."

Harriet stared out the window. *Where are you, Petey?*

Twenty minutes later, Harriet stood on Gwen's doorstep, knocking on the pink door.

Van had dropped her off on his way back to the station, assuring her that he would continue to make inquiries into Petey's whereabouts. "Don't you worry, Doc. We'll find the little guy sooner or later."

Harriet nodded. "I hope so. I want to find him before the London dog show. Gwen has her heart set on winning the competition this year. Of course, that's much less important to her than finding Petey, but I'd like for all of this to disrupt her life as little as possible."

Now Harriet glanced at the narrow strip of grass behind the wrought iron gate and wondered if Petey had been afraid when the stranger snatched him from the yard. Had the dog been gently coaxed with a treat, or grabbed forcibly? Petey was friendly and used to strangers. He might have gone easily enough.

When no one came to the door, Harriet knocked again.

A neighbor across the narrow street poked her head out an open window and called, "She's not at home, love. She went out about half an hour ago."

"Thanks," Harriet called back with a smile.

Glancing at her watch, she decided to walk to the Happy Cup Tearoom for some refreshment. She wasn't yet hungry enough for lunch, but a cup of tea and a pastry would hit the spot. She strode along the winding street, checking her phone as she went. The clinic was open that morning, but she had no appointments scheduled. She had no missed messages about veterinary emergencies, so Harriet decided she could afford to relax a little and enjoy her Saturday.

It would be easier if a small dog wasn't missing, possibly injured, or in danger.

Harriet entered the tea shop, smoothing her wind-tousled hair. She took a deep breath, inhaling the tantalizing aromas. As she glanced around for an available seat, she caught sight of Gwen sitting with Aunt Jinny at a corner table.

They noticed her at the same time, and her aunt waved her over. "Harriet, join us."

"I don't want to intrude," Harriet said, pausing beside the table.

Gwen gestured to an empty chair. "Nonsense. Have a seat."

Harriet sat down. She knew without even asking that Petey had not yet been found, based on Gwen's furrowed brow and pinched expression. After the waitress had taken Harriet's order, Harriet said to Gwen, "No news about Petey, I suppose."

Gwen shook her head, her shoulders drooping.

"Not even a ransom note, which might give us additional information," Aunt Jinny said.

Harriet raised her eyebrows in surprise. "Do you think someone took Petey for money?"

Gwen shrugged. "I don't know what to think. Until we know more, I feel it's best to be prepared for anything. Though given the lack of a ransom note, I am less and less inclined to think this is about money."

"Gwen has filled me in on everything regarding Petey's disappearance," Aunt Jinny said. "I'm guessing you've spent the morning on this."

"Yes." The waitress returned with her order. Harriet admired the turf cake, also called a fat rascal. The little cake, served with a dollop of thick cream on the side, was warm and fresh from the oven, just the way she liked it. During her childhood visits with her grandfather, Harriet had enjoyed many of the short-crust pastries mixed with dried fruit, butter, and sugar and flavored with nutmeg, cinnamon, and lemon zest. The traditional Yorkshire cake was one of her favorite treats.

Harriet savored a bite then said, "Van has been going door-to-door making inquiries. I went with him to Rupert Decker's place."

"And?" Gwen prompted, leaning forward slightly in her chair.

"And I think we can scratch him off our list of possible suspects," Harriet told her. "His son, Clarence, too. They were playing darts at the Crow's Nest, so they both have an alibi, and there was no obvious sign of Petey. Van is going to follow up on the alibi, but that one is too easy to check for them to lie about it." The Crow's Nest was a local pub that had some of the best comfort food in the village.

"Who else is on the list?" Aunt Jinny wanted to know.

"Alistair Marling, I suppose." Gwen peered into her empty tea-cup and said rather wistfully, "But I don't believe he really did take Petey, even though he is quite tall. Jane insists the abductor was a very tall man."

"I have a hard time imagining Alistair doing such a thing," Aunt Jinny said. "How did he end up on your list of suspects?"

Harriet supplied the answer. "Because he's tall for one thing, and apparently, he's having financial difficulties."

"So he kidnapped Petey for monetary reasons?" Her aunt looked dubious.

Gwen said, "That's possible, I suppose, but again, there's been no ransom note. I couldn't afford to pay much anyway. Any local would know that."

Harriet sipped her coffee and broke off a piece of her pastry. She didn't want to mention the possibility that Alistair or someone else could have stolen the dog to sell to a puppy mill. She made a mental note to ask Van if such places were a problem here in England.

"Who else is on the suspect list?" Aunt Jinny asked as she refilled Gwen's cup from the small brown teapot on the table.

"I don't know who's on Van's official list, but mine includes Billy Brindle," Gwen said.

"Why him?" Aunt Jinny probed.

"He owns a champion chow. Tamzin Pickers suggested that Billy might have taken Petey so his dog would have a better chance of winning the championship in London," Harriet explained.

"But Billy is at university," Aunt Jinny said. "Do we know for a fact that he's entered his dog in the London show?"

"No, and I'm not sure how we could check," Harriet replied. "Since we have no evidence, all of this is simply speculation."

"Seems like a rather desperate thing to do," Aunt Jinny mused. "It would certainly be poor sportsmanship."

"Do you know Billy?" Harriet asked.

"No," her aunt said. "But I know his mother, Rose." Then her eyes lit up. "Why don't you and I go pay her a visit?"

Harriet arched her eyebrows. "Right now?'

"Right now," her aunt said, dabbing her lips with her napkin. "We need to find Petey before the dog show, don't we?"

CHAPTER NINE

A re you sure about this?" Harriet gave her aunt a dubious glance as they stood on the narrow front step of the Brindle home. It was a three-story house, white with black shutters, and so near the shore that she could hear the noisy chorus of the gulls.

"No." Aunt Jinny lifted the tarnished brass knocker that resembled a gargoyle and rapped it against the door. "But it's worth a try, isn't it?"

They'd left her aunt's vehicle at a car park and walked the short distance to the Brindle home. Her aunt carried a pink-and-white cake box from the bakery.

"We're helping a friend find her lost dog," Aunt Jinny said. "No harm in asking questions."

Harriet licked her lips, more from nervousness than anything else. She'd never met Rose Brindle before and didn't know how the woman would react to their questions. Still, they needed to speak with as many residents as possible. "Can you tell me anything about her?"

"Rose is married to an electrician who works for a firm over in Scarborough. I doubt Billy will be at home, since he's taking classes at the university in Leeds. But who knows?"

A woman with brown hair and red-rimmed glasses opened the door. She wore tan khakis and a red turtleneck. Her face lit up when she recognized Aunt Jinny. "Dr. Garrett, what a pleasant surprise."

"Hello, Rose. This is my niece, Harriet Bailey."

Rose turned her smile on Harriet. "The lady vet. I've heard about you. You've taken over Old Doc Bailey's practice, I understand. He was your grandfather, right?"

"That's right. Nice to meet you, Mrs. Brindle," Harriet replied with a smile of her own.

"Please call me Rose."

"And this curd tart is for you, Rose," Aunt Jinny said, presenting her with the bakery box. A Yorkshire curd tart had a rich filling made of cottage cheese, which the British often called "curd cheese," dried fruit such as currants, and spices.

"Well, how lovely." Rose's eyes danced with pleasure. "Where are my manners? Won't you come in?" She stepped aside to allow them into the foyer and indicated a sunny room to their right. "I'll just put this in the kitchen and join you in the sitting room. The kettle is on, so we can enjoy a cup of tea."

"Oh, please don't bother for our sakes," Aunt Jinny told her. "We've come from the Happy Cup, as you may have guessed from the box, so we just had tea."

"All right then. I'll be right there," Rose said. "Please make yourselves comfortable."

Harriet followed her aunt into the sitting room. It felt small because it overflowed with potted ferns, a colorful array of African violets, and other houseplants. An aquarium of tropical fish had pride of place in one corner. Although a large window faced the sea, Harriet noted no ocean view. Instead, the Brindles had a view of their neighbors' equally tall house and the climbing ivy on the walls.

Sitting next to her aunt on an overstuffed sofa, Harriet decided it was a cheery, comfortable room with a lived-in feeling. She liked it.

When Rose returned, she sat down in a cushioned rocking chair across from them. "How are you finding our village?" she asked, addressing Harriet. "Are you settling in? Making friends?"

"I love it," Harriet answered truthfully. "Everyone has been so kind. I feel right at home."

"I have no pets except the fish." Rose indicated the tank in the corner of the room. "So I've had no reason to make your acquaintance in a professional way. But I'm happy to do so now as a neighbor."

Harriet gave her a warm smile. She liked the woman and hoped her son had nothing to do with Petey's abduction.

Rose asked, "So what's the occasion for this visit? Are you collecting for a charity? The PDSA fund, perhaps? Dr. Bailey, have you heard about the PDSA?"

"I learned about the organization this week, actually," Harriet replied. "It's a charity for sick and injured animals, right?"

"That's right," Rose said. "I've donated in the past, and my son, Billy, has volunteered with them. He hasn't had much time for it lately, as he's attending university in Leeds."

"I've been doing a bit of research about the Dickin Medal," Harriet said. "Are you familiar with that?"

"Certainly. They started giving out medals to animals who helped with the war effort during World War II. Then the practice fell by the wayside for several years, but Billy told me they've revived the tradition again."

"How is Billy?" Aunt Jinny asked.

Harriet fought a grin. It was hardly a smooth transition, but she knew her aunt was eager to get to the point of their visit.

"Billy is busy but well," Rose replied. "Medical courses, you know."

"I remember those days well," Harriet said. "It must leave him precious little time for other pursuits. For example, I understand he owns a dog that has won a blue ribbon or trophy or some such."

Rose lifted her chin, pride evident on her face. "That would be Mitzi. She's a chow. Billy is so good with animals. He's done a fine job training her. And she has indeed won a prize or two." Rose hopped up to retrieve a photo from the mantel and brought it to Harriet. "This is Billy with his dog. He has Mitzi with him over in Leeds."

The photo revealed a very tall young man with dark hair and a bright smile standing next to a fine chow. Two men appeared to be presenting Billy with a trophy. He towered over the other two men. Harriet couldn't help but recall yet again Jane Birtwhistle's testimony about the very tall man who'd taken Petey from Gwen's garden.

She took her time admiring the photo before handing it to her aunt. "Such a handsome young man and a beautiful dog. You must be so proud," Harriet said with a smile.

Rose beamed. "I am."

"Billy is so much taller than I remember," Aunt Jinny noted, handing her the photo.

"Six foot four if he's an inch. Gets his height from his father's side of the family. Viking blood somewhere along the line, they say." Then her expression became more somber as she seemed to realize something. "If you've come to ask about seeing Mitzi at your clinic, Dr. Bailey, I'm sorry. Billy takes Mitzi to a vet in Leeds. He rents a house there, you see. He doesn't come home too often."

Harriet gave Rose a warm smile to put her at ease. "Not to worry. I'm glad Mitzi has someone to see to her health and welfare. Happy pet, happy pet owner, I always say. And she'll need to be at her best if Billy's entering her in the dog show in London in a couple weeks. I imagine that's easier with a vet local to where he lives and goes to school."

"Unfortunately, he and Mitzi won't be competing in London," Rose said. "Besides his courses at university, he's also working part-time in a pet store. Working and studying are about all he has time for these days. It's a shame that we won't see a local face at the London show."

Aunt Jinny pounced on the opening. "Actually, that's why we've come. Our friend Gwen Higginbottom means to compete in that show, but her Scottish terrier went missing Thursday night. We're making inquiries throughout the village, hoping that someone may have seen the little dog. He goes by the name of Petey and is very friendly." Aunt Jinny took one of Gwen's flyers from her purse and handed it to Rose.

"I'm sorry to hear he's missing," Rose said, glancing at the flyer. "But I don't know how I can help you. I haven't seen him."

"You could keep watch for him when you're out and about," Harriet suggested. "Or if you hear of someone who has found a little black terrier running loose in the street, please let us know."

"Have you called the dogcatcher?" Rose asked, lacing her fingers in her lap.

"Yes, Rand Cromwell is on the lookout, and so are the police," Aunt Jinny assured her. "We're hoping to find Petey before the show in London. Gwen has entered him in the competition."

"I wish her the best of luck," Rose said. When Aunt Jinny stood up, Rose did too. Harriet followed their lead.

"We appreciate any help you can give us," Aunt Jinny added.

"I'll ask around," Rose promised. "And thank you for the tart. My Ned will be delighted to have that with his supper. He's fond of his sweets."

"Aren't we all?" Harriet asked with a chuckle.

Rose laughed as she walked them to the door. Once again, she wished them well in finding Petey.

Harriet scratched the very tall Billy Brindle off her mental list of possible suspects. Before heading back to the car park, she said, "How about some fish and chips? My treat."

"Sounds good," her aunt agreed, falling into step beside her. Once they were well away from the house, she added, "I don't think Billy Brindle is involved."

"I don't think so either. But what's your reason?" Harriet asked, watching her step on the cobbled sidewalk.

"It's not likely that a busy university student drove all the way from Leeds to White Church in the pouring rain to snatch Petey from Gwen's yard. What sort of motive would he have for all of that? He's not competing against her in London." Aunt Jinny opened the door to Cliffside Chippy, which had the best fish and chips in the area.

The conversation went on hold until they were both seated on a bench on the shore, watching the surf and enjoying hot fried fish and french fries. It was sunny and pleasantly brisk. The tide was coming in. The gray-blue waves whipped the shore and retreated again. The sunlight appeared muted, like an impressionist painting, and sea grass waved in the October breeze.

"Okay, I'll agree it's unlikely that Billy Brindle kidnapped Petey," Harriet said, taking up the conversation again. "But if we were the police, we wouldn't eliminate the possibility until we'd verified his whereabouts on the night in question."

Aunt Jinny chewed a fry. "But we aren't the police. Are you going to ask Van to follow up?"

"No. I think we should pursue another course of action. Although Billy is tall, we only have Jane's impression that the culprit was a tall man. Besides, how tall is tall? Jane is short, so anyone might seem tall to her."

They ate in silence for a while. Harriet watched people strolling the beach bundled up in sweatshirts and jackets. The brisk breeze stirred her hair, carrying the scent of fried fish and the sea. She brushed a strand from her cheek as she listened to the raucous chorus of the gulls.

"Who else is on the list?" Aunt Jinny asked.

"Alistair Marling," Harriet replied.

Aunt Jinny snorted. "I realize he's a tall man, tall enough to stand out in a crowd. But you really think a middle-aged insurance salesman would snatch Gwen's dog? As I said before, I don't see Alistair strolling through the rain in yellow boots. We can't accuse a man simply because he's tall and can be relentless about his sales."

Harriet shrugged. "Stranger things have happened. We also can't clear him because we can't picture him in the right outfit."

Before Aunt Jinny could respond, Harriet's cell phone buzzed. She fumbled in her purse to retrieve it, hoping there wasn't an animal-related emergency. She was enjoying her leisurely Saturday.

It was Gwen Higginbottom. "Harriet, when I arrived home, I had a letter in the post. It's about Petey."

London
March 1941

Dear Malcolm,

Winter has come and gone. Weather's warming up a bit. Not much greenery around here, and I surely miss the sea.

The Dig for Victory campaign is alive and well here, with everyone growing their own vegetables and such. Everyone is planting seeds. You're not the only one help-ing to feed the nation. Open spaces everywhere are being transformed into allotments, including private gardens and public parks. The lawns outside the Tower of London are being turned into vegetable patches too. The Ministry of Agriculture reps have been handing out leaflets telling folks what to grow and how. Old Mrs. Fishkill down the street has even planted lettuce and radishes in her win-dow boxes. I hope for her sake the bombing doesn't put an end to her hard work.

Never doubt you're doing important work, Mick, with the farming and all. Our soldiers have to eat. We've all got to keep up our strength. Are you getting any help from those Land Girls I read about in the Daily Mail? Garrick and I had a bit of a laugh just thinking of all the shop girls trading in their high heels for a pair of wellies and going out to the country to milk cows or drive a tractor.

Do you have any city youngsters moving into York? Lots of parents here are still sending their kids to the country to get away from the bombing. Some are even shipping the youngsters all the way to Canada. Would you and Penny even consider doing such a thing? I don't think I'd like that. I'm not a father, of course, so I can't really say what I'd do given that situation.

But who's to say the youngsters will be safe in the countryside? They might not be bombing York and Scarborough today, but I reckon they'll get around to it sooner or later. And what about all those German U-boats with their torpedoes? What happens to all the little ones sailing off to Canada then? It's a terrible decision that parents must make. They want to keep their youngsters safe. I'm glad I'm not in their shoes. Tough times all around.

You asked in your letter about the bombing. Tired to death of it, I am. But it doesn't happen as frequently here as before. Hitler's picking on Liverpool and other cities. We all must hang on. I still have my health, for which I am grateful, and the sure knowledge that I'm needed. Someone must remove the dead and save the survivors. We're desperately shorthanded. Garrick says the ARP would take on Jack the Ripper if he'd agree to work nights and days.

Some say in another week or so, Churchill will give up. Others say we should have listened to Mosely, that folks didn't want another war. Well, we've got one, whether we want it or not. Call me a fool, but I don't like the idea of surrendering, not when we've worked so hard and come this far. The idea of giving up doesn't sit right with me, not with all that's at stake. Losing this war would mean losing our very souls.

Rip is still with me, doing his bit for king and country. I thought he'd have gone off by now to find his family, but so far, he's sticking like glue. He's really attached himself to me, and I value his company. He's proved his worth time and again. And what ears he's got! Despite all the noise during a bombing raid and men shouting and sirens blaring, Rip can hear a whimper, a groan, a cry beneath the rubble. Then he starts digging right away.

We've come to trust him completely, Garrick and me. The men on the team are coming to do so as well. He digs and digs until his paws are bloody and sore, and he's saved more lives than I can count. He cocks his head to one side and listens. When he starts digging with that dogged ferocity, we come alongside. He hasn't been wrong yet. "Look sharp!" I'll call out, and then we all start digging where Rip digs. Hastings, the copper I mentioned, is looking into getting some leather booties or something for his poor feet.

A couple of nights ago, we spent hours shoveling through the rubble of a collapsed apartment building. The cleanup crew arrived with their lorry, and we were calling it quits so they could carry off the debris. But Rip wasn't having it. He whined and kept staring at a spot we'd already checked. He wouldn't budge, no matter how many times I told him there was no one there. Finally, one of our mates brought a ladder and climbed up. Sure enough, he found a man on a top floor ledge pinned by debris— unconscious, but very much alive.

It turns out the man was a butcher. He came around yesterday with a bag of sausages and a couple of sirloins. He wanted to thank us for coming to his rescue and said no rationing regulations would stop him from doing so. We had a great tea break that day, I can tell you.

The Good Lord has given this scruffy little mutt a real talent for rescue. It is often said that God has a purpose for us all. I reckon it's so. Rip isn't the only dog out among the rubble searching for survivors. There are others. In fact, the Civil Defense is setting up a school to train dogs to do what Rip is doing naturally. That's something.

When we're tired and want to give up, we take our cue from Rip. He located two little girls in the rubble of a bombed house last week. We'd marked it as clear, thinking the residents had sought refuge in the bomb shelter at the end of the street once the warning sirens went off. Don't know where the mum and dad were, but the two girls were alone in the house. Rip knew it and got to work digging. We joined him, giving it our all. I removed broken bricks so fast I started breathing hard and got a stitch in my side. I could hear Rip panting, and Garrick's breath came in ragged gasps. He's not a young man after all.

Anyway, we saved those little girls, thanks to Rip. The poor things never said a word. They just stared ahead at nothing in particular. No moaning, no crying for their mum. Garrick said he's seen soldiers in the first war doing the same. He called it shell shock. It all but broke my heart. Hastings and another constable carried them to the nearest rest center. Children shouldn't have to endure things like this. I got queasy just thinking about what might have happened to them if we hadn't listened to Rip.

Some say the war will be over this summer. I'm not so sure. When Garrick heard the so-called prediction, he said, "And pigs might fly." Well, here's hoping they are right anyway. Hoping and praying. The end of this war cannot come too soon.

Your weary cousin,

Brad

PS. I forgot to mention, I went to a dance last Saturday night. Can you believe it, with my having two left feet and all? Rip wasn't keen about my going, but Garrick said he'd keep an eye on him for me. Not one of the women there paid any attention to me at all, and I couldn't blame them. They all wanted to dance with those boys in blue—the RAF airmen and even the ground crew. But I didn't mind. I'm not keen on dancing anyway. Had a soda and watched from a corner table. It was a change from my usual routine. Might even go again.

CHAPTER TEN

It doesn't sound like a ransom note, does it?" Gwen perched on the edge of a straight-backed chair with an embroidered cushion. She twisted her hands in her lap, her eyes wide and anxious.

Harriet and Aunt Jinny sat next to each other on the floral sofa, studying the letter Gwen had received in the afternoon post. "It doesn't sound like one to me," Harriet agreed. "There's no demand for money and no threats to harm Petey if you don't pay up. I'm glad for that part at least."

Aunt Jinny read the words aloud. "'Your dog is so handsome and sweet too. I know you must miss him. He will return home soon.'" Glancing at Harriet, she asked, "What sort of dognapper writes a note reassuring the owner that her dog will be returned and doesn't ask for anything?"

Harriet glanced at Gwen, whose eyes glistened with unshed tears. Harriet couldn't decide whether the note was meant to be reassuring, or if it contained a veiled threat of some kind. She decided to keep the latter thought to herself. It would upset Gwen more than she was already, and with no actual proof.

"I need to call the detective constable again. His line was busy. Do you think a letter demanding money will follow this one?" Gwen pointed to the note that Aunt Jinny had placed on the low teakwood coffee table.

"I couldn't say," Aunt Jinny replied. "Did anything strike you as odd about it, Harriet?"

"I think the handwriting is rather childish," Harriet said. "It's printed, for one thing. The writing slants to the left, which could indicate a left-handed writer, and the letters are unusually large."

The letter had arrived in a self-sealing security envelope. The note was printed using blue ink from a ballpoint pen on the plain white paper generally used in a computer printer. There was nothing distinctive about either the paper or the envelope that would make them easy to trace.

Harriet tapped the page. "It seems odd to write on printer paper rather than typing the note and printing it off."

"The sender might not have had a computer or printer. Perhaps it was a child," Gwen suggested.

"Most kids have access to computers at school if not at home," Harriet pointed out. "I wouldn't say for certain this was written by a child."

"I think an adult wrote the note trying to disguise his handwriting," Aunt Jinny said. "He thinks he's being clever, even sneaky, by intentionally trying to mislead us."

"It was postmarked in Scarborough," Harriet said. "There's nothing special about the postage stamp either. Not that I can see anyway."

"Does that mean Petey is in Scarborough?" Gwen asked, her voice thick with emotion.

"Not necessarily," Aunt Jinny told her. "As I recall, all mail posted here is sent to Scarborough for processing and then returned here to be delivered."

"That doesn't sound very efficient," Harriet said.

"The postal center there is automated. Every piece of mail is processed and postmarked by machines to save time and money," Aunt Jinny explained.

Harriet pursed her lips as she reread the note. "I'm surprised the sender used the word *please*. 'Please don't worry about your dog.' I would think that's not how criminals usually talk to their victims. Although I'll admit I'm no expert."

"I don't understand it," Gwen muttered. "Nothing about this letter makes sense to me."

"If the person's planning to return the dog, why steal Petey in the first place?" Aunt Jinny added.

Gwen lurched to her feet and paced back and forth in front of the small fireplace, wringing her hands as she did so. "I couldn't begin to guess."

Harriet watched her with dismay. The poor woman was over-wrought. Harriet didn't know how she could help or what she could say to ease her burden. As she contemplated the problem, she noted there was no fire in the hearth or any of the usual fireplace tools such as a poker, tongs, or broom. No evidence of soot or ash. She assumed the fireplace had not been used in years. Dog show tro-phies, ribbons, and framed photos of Petey dotted the mantel. Maybe Gwen didn't use the fireplace for its intended purpose in order to protect those items.

Gwen faced the two of them. "I'm scared. I don't know why he was taken or when they'll bring him back—if the note is even telling the truth about that."

"Gwen, do sit down," Aunt Jinny urged. "We must remain calm and think this through. Try calling Van again."

"Not yet." Gwen returned to her chair. "I want to finish talking it through with the two of you first. Do you think the constable can get fingerprints from the note or the envelope? DNA maybe? Any clues at all?"

"I doubt it," Harriet said. "The three of us have probably ruined any chance of that."

"The tone of the note really puzzles me," Aunt Jinny said. "Perhaps the sender is trying to put you at your ease, not wanting you to worry about Petey's well-being. It's as if he's attempting to be considerate of how you must be feeling as a dog owner."

"Considerate?" Gwen snapped. "I would hardly agree. If he wanted to be considerate, he wouldn't have taken Petey in the first place."

Harriet spotted the glint of anger in Gwen's eyes. The woman was exhibiting a little spirit at last. Harriet felt a surge of relief. Any emotion was better than despair.

"You're sure it's not Rupert Decker or his son?" Gwen demanded of Harriet. "I can't say I know Clarence well enough to make such a judgment call. Are you sure neither of them took my dog?"

"Quite sure. As I mentioned before, they have an alibi for the time in question." Harriet felt certain Van would confirm this sooner or later. He might have already done so, and he was under no obligation to update her. "And the detective constable and I saw no evidence of Petey at the Decker home when we were there."

"Then what about Billy Brindle?" Gwen pressed. "You visited Rose Brindle today, didn't you?"

"Yes, we did," Aunt Jinny told her. "But Harriet and I feel certain that Billy had nothing to do with Petey's disappearance."

"But you don't really know," Gwen argued.

"We know as well as we can without having the official authority to verify alibis," Aunt Jinny replied. She shared what Rose had told them about Billy's busy schedule. "And he hasn't entered his dog in the London competition, so he has no reason to want to keep you and Petey out of the ring."

Harriet said nothing. They'd already gone over this. She didn't believe Billy had taken Petey, but she had no definite proof. Just because his mother told them he was too busy with school and work didn't mean Billy hadn't taken the time to drive over from Leeds to steal Gwen's dog. And even though he hadn't entered his own dog in the London competition, that didn't mean he might not be willing to do a favor for a friend by keeping Petey out of the running.

The sole comfort in that scenario was knowing that Billy was a dog lover. If he had abducted Petey—and that was a big *if*—Harriet doubted he would hurt the little terrier in any way. In fact, Billy might be the sort of person who would send a reassuring note with the words *please don't worry*. But she decided not to share these thoughts with Gwen either. Best to keep such thoughts to herself. She didn't want to encourage the woman to go around pointing fingers.

"Then who stole my Petey?" Gwen asked. "If it wasn't one of the Deckers or Billy Brindle, that leaves Alistair Marling. He's the other tall man Jane Birtwhistle thought of."

Aunt Jinny laughed. "We've been over this, Gwen. Alistair's hardly the type to dash about in the rain while wearing yellow wellies. Nor is he the type to carry off a dog. It would be quite out of character for him to do so. What possible motive could he have? Besides, such antics as dognapping would be bad for business, and if Alistair is anything, he's a dedicated businessman. He wouldn't do anything to jeopardize that. It's ridiculous to even consider him as a possible suspect. For all we know, the dognapper is a complete stranger to you and the rest of us as well."

"Alistair is tall, and Jane insisted the man she saw was remarkably so," Gwen argued.

Harriet resisted the urge to say that Jane's list of suspects was a flimsy one. Besides, as she and Aunt Jinny had discussed, what Jane considered tall might not be the same as what anyone else would. Harriet finally said, "I find it hard to believe that Alistair would write a note like this. As Aunt Jinny said, it seems so out of character."

"But we don't know for sure," Gwen insisted.

Harriet closed her eyes. How many times would they go over this?

"We don't know for sure, that's true," Aunt Jinny conceded.

"Then we're back right where we started," Gwen said. "Nowhere. Haven't a clue about the culprit. So what do we do now?"

Harriet hesitated. She considered the possibility that someone needed to speak with Jane again. Maybe now that a little time had passed, she might remember something else, something that hadn't seemed important at the time.

"You need to call Van and show him the note," Aunt Jinny told Gwen again. "Then we need to sit and wait patiently. Who knows? The writer of this note might send another one, explaining what's going on and why he took Petey. Perhaps even when he'll return Petey."

"Do you think the man who took Petey intends to return him before the dog show?" Gwen asked. "Should I cancel my hotel reservation? Should I withdraw Petey from the competition?"

"Sit tight. Don't do anything yet," Harriet advised. "You still have over a week before the big show. Let's see what happens in the next few days."

"I agree," Aunt Jinny said, reaching over to give Gwen's hand a reassuring squeeze.

Gwen heaved a sigh. "Do you think the man is taking good care of Petey?"

Harriet was determined to go on thinking positively—and praying. "The note seems to indicate that Petey will be returned soon. And that's a good thing. Right?"

"But when?" Gwen asked. "When will that be? How soon is 'soon'?"

And much as she would have liked to give that answer, Harriet hadn't the foggiest idea.

CHAPTER ELEVEN

Harriet had the opportunity to speak with Jane Birtwhistle the very next day after the Sunday morning church service. She watched as Jane stood beside Gwen, who was surrounded by well-wishers all expressing their sympathy at Petey's disappearance. Gwen appeared stoic for a few minutes, but then she burst into tears, apparently touched by so much sympathy, and hurried away to her car.

"No word yet about Gwen's little dog?" Doreen asked Harriet, pausing on the sidewalk.

Mindful of Doreen's husband and their passel of youngsters eager to escape the cold, brisk day with their warm home and waiting meal, Harriet shook her head. "I'll fill you in later." She hastened to join Aunt Jinny. As she passed the south end of the church, she noticed that someone had been turning over the rich, dark soil to make a long flower bed of sorts, probably for bulbs. It was much too late in the season to plant anything else.

Aunt Jinny had invited both Harriet and Jane to her home after church for lunch. Finding out that Pastor Fitzwilliam "Will" Knight didn't have any plans, she invited him too. The three women arrived at the house first, where Aunt Jinny's home was filled with the aromas of a roast in the slow cooker with onions, potatoes, and carrots smothered in a creamy brown gravy. She removed yeast rolls from the oven while the minister parked outside and made his way up to the front door of Aunt Jinny's cottage with a long-legged stride.

Harriet met him at the door. Will was tall and quite good-looking. His cheeks appeared flushed from the cold. He had a charming smile that quickly put others at ease. And as his smile was contagious, she returned it.

"Sorry I'm late," he said. "A young couple stayed after to make arrangements for premarital counseling."

"Oh, wedding bells for some blessed couple," Jane said as Aunt Jinny ushered them to the table. "How exciting."

"Anyone I know?" Aunt Jinny asked, placing the basket of hot rolls beside the bowl of vegetables.

Will shared the names of the happy couple, but Harriet didn't know them personally. She had a vague recollection of a willowy redheaded woman and a broad farmer with a slight moustache.

Aunt Jinny asked Will to say grace, which he did.

While passing the serving platter and bowls around, Harriet glanced across the table at Will. Her aunt occasionally tried to play matchmaker with her and the handsome pastor. She seemed determined that Harriet and Will spend time together.

Aunt Jinny meant well, but Harriet wasn't sure she was ready for a relationship. She enjoyed Will's company and certainly found him to be a good and attractive man. But she'd been taken by surprise when her fellow veterinarian back in the States, Dustin Stewart, broke off their engagement. Between the emotional distress of calling off the wedding and the extra stress of working in the same office as Dustin, Harriet had been happy to escape across the ocean to Cobble Hill Farm. "Once bitten, twice shy" was an old saying her grandfather had used occasionally. It seemed appropriate, as Harriet certainly meant to look before she leaped next time. If there even was a next time.

Will glanced up from his plate and caught Harriet staring at him. His hazel eyes twinkled, and he smiled.

She felt her cheeks warm and quickly turned her attention to a chunk of roasted potato on her plate.

"Pastor Will, I certainly appreciated your sermon this morning," Jane said, taking his focus from Harriet. "You gave us a lot to think about."

Harriet agreed with her. Will had preached on the parable of the great banquet from the book of Luke. He'd encouraged his congregation to extend hospitality and friendship to those society overlooked for one reason or another, and to show God's love in ways that might take them out of their comfort zone.

"Thank you," Will replied. "You can't go wrong with one of the Lord's many parables. They contain endless wisdom." He toasted Aunt Jinny with a forkful of food. "This is delicious, Jinny. You're quite the cook."

Aunt Jinny smiled as she passed around her homemade applesauce. "That's kind of you, Pastor, but isn't there a proverb in the Bible about how even bad food tastes delicious in good company?"

Will laughed. "Perhaps you're thinking of Proverbs 15:17, which says a small serving of vegetables with love is better than a fattened calf with hatred."

Everyone laughed, and then Jane said, "Pastor, did you hear that Gwen Higginbottom's Scottish terrier was abducted on Thursday night?"

"Yes, I understand it happened while she was at the church during choir practice," Will answered. "Such a shame."

"I saw it happen," Jane informed him. "Unfortunately, I didn't realize what I was seeing at the time, or we might not be so far behind the dognapper now."

Arching an eyebrow, Will asked, "What did you see?"

Jane related her story. Harriet listened carefully but heard no new details. When Jane was through, she said to Harriet, "Perhaps you should tell the pastor about our list of suspects."

Will grinned at Harriet. "I should have known you'd already be knee-deep in an investigation like this. What have you learned?"

Harriet hesitated. She didn't want to be too frank in front of Jane Birtwhistle. She feared the older woman might take something out of context and fan it into a flame of rumor with very little truth. When she glanced sidelong at Aunt Jinny, the unspoken warning in her aunt's expression confirmed that her caution was well-founded.

However, at the same time, she didn't want Will to think she didn't trust him. She wanted to confide in him, to be open and completely honest, but perhaps not at this time.

After taking a sip of her water, she replied matter-of-factly, "I'm a bit befuddled, honestly. Jane said she saw a tall man carrying Petey—that's the missing dog—out of Gwen's garden through the gate. There are so many tall men in White Church Bay. Without more to go on, I'm afraid the police investigation can only go so far."

"What about Rupert Decker or his son, Clarence?" Jane asked.

"But why on earth would either one of them take a dog?" Will asked, perplexed.

"Clarence takes in all kinds of injured and stray animals," Harriet said. "However, I don't believe either he or his father took Petey. Both have an ironclad alibi." She didn't want to say anything about the possibility of Rupert taking revenge on Gwen with Jane listening. "They were at the Crow's Nest playing darts on the night Petey went missing." At least, Van hadn't told her that he'd learned otherwise.

Jane was not to be deterred. "And then there's Billy Brindle. He's quite tall—exceptionally so."

Aunt Jinny chimed in, "It wasn't Billy either." She didn't bother to explain how she knew that or why. Apparently, she also wanted to give Jane as little to run with as possible.

Harriet felt a sudden weariness. They seemed to be stuck in a rut, going over the same conjectures over and over again. She turned her attention to the gravy-soaked piece of beef speared on her fork. Would they ever catch the culprit? Or would they have to wait until Petey was safely returned, as the note hinted he would be?

Jane went on. "Alistair Marling is tall. He might be the one."

Will chuckled. "No, I think we can safely eliminate Alistair. I can't imagine him sneaking around in yellow boots and rain gear on a rainy night. He wouldn't be caught dead dressed like that."

Harriet grinned at Aunt Jinny, who smiled, probably thinking that she'd been saying the same thing all along. Now that Harriet really considered it, she had to agree. Alistair might be annoyingly pushy, but one couldn't fault his sense of style. With his wide smile, well-groomed hair, and immaculate clothing, he could have stepped right out of a fashion magazine. He would surely opt for sophisticated rain gear from a posh shop and consider the yellow getup garish.

"Besides," Will went on, "I happen to know he has a serious allergy to pet dander—dogs, cats, guinea pigs, the lot. It's not a secret, so I'm not breaking any confidences to tell you that." Putting down his fork, he turned to Jane. "Did you know that he rarely calls on people inside their homes to make his sales pitch, especially when they have pets? He'll go door-to-door, but he usually stays outside, and in general he prefers to meet with potential clients at his office in the village. He can't risk being exposed."

Jane looked a bit uncomfortable. "Well, I didn't say it *was* him," she said grudgingly. "I just said it *could* be him."

Harriet cleared her throat. "He was here on Thursday evening." She glanced at her aunt for confirmation. "I remember you said that he didn't come inside?"

"That's right," Aunt Jinny said. "He handed me a packet of information at the door."

With a shrug, Harriet said, "I suppose that's why he's never visited me at the clinic or my house to follow up on his sales pitch."

After passing around the basket of rolls again, Aunt Jinny said, "Harriet, tell them about the note Gwen received yesterday."

Jane gasped and placed a hand on her chest. "I knew it! A ransom note."

"No, it was practically an apology," Harriet told her. "I took a picture of it with my cell phone, if you want to read it later." She could see the note in her mind's eye. "Basically, it just said how sweet Petey is and that he would be returned soon."

"Well, I never," Jane declared softly. She dabbed at her lips with her napkin. "I don't know what to make of that. Truly I don't."

"Neither do I," Will said with a puzzled frown. "Sounds a bit like the dognapper is suffering from a guilty conscience and that he intends to return Petey sooner or later. I suppose that's good news."

"He should have a guilty conscience," Jane said indignantly. "After all, 'thou shalt not steal.'"

"That's right, but we need to let God be the ultimate judge. Only He knows what a person has in their heart," Will reminded her gently. "Anything remarkable about the note or the envelope?"

"Nothing," Harriet told him. "And there's no return address to give us a clue about the sender."

"But why abduct the dog in the first place if he intends to return him without asking for anything?" Will mused.

"That's the million-dollar question, isn't it?" Aunt Jinny asked.

Harriet's cell phone rang. She looked down and saw that it was the clinic's emergency number. She knew everyone there understood why she carried her phone 24/7, so she said, "I'm sorry, I need to take this," and rose from the table. She and Aunt Jinny had shared many stories with each other of interrupted parties, dinners, and shows.

Harriet moved into the hallway to take the call. A couple had found a stray cat yowling in distress in an alley behind the hardware store. "It's covered with something that smells like petrol," the caller told her. "Can we bring him to your clinic? We have no idea how to help the poor thing."

"Of course," Harriet replied. She gave the woman directions and then scooped up her purse, sliding her phone inside the outer pocket before returning to the dining room. "I'm sorry, Aunt Jinny, I need to leave. There's an emergency involving a cat."

"Oh, what a shame. I made a chocolate cake for dessert," her aunt said.

"Save a piece for me," Harriet said. "I'll come by later and have tea with you. I love your chocolate cake."

"How about I go with you?" Will asked. "Polly won't be there, and you might need an extra pair of hands."

Pleasantly surprised by the offer, Harriet agreed immediately. "That's a great idea, and I'd really appreciate it. The woman said she and her husband only have enough time to drop the cat off, so you're right—I might need your help."

She said goodbye to Jane then kissed her aunt on the cheek and thanked her for a lovely meal.

Shortly afterward, she greeted Mr. and Mrs. Watkins at the door of her clinic and accepted a cardboard box from them. "It's scared to death, poor thing," Mr. Watkins said. "We don't know how to care for it, but we figured you'd know what to do." He gave Harriet a nod and eyed Will's clerical collar with mild curiosity.

Harriet peered into the box. Their assessment was right. The cat reeked of gasoline. Its green eyes were wide with terror, its gray fur sticking up like porcupine quills. It quivered with fright and cowered in the corner of the box. Harriet felt a surge of sympathy for the scared little thing. She had to get it cleaned up as quickly as possible, before it tried to groom off the toxic substance—if it hadn't already. She would also need to check for signs of that.

"I tried to wipe him down with a kitchen towel, but that won't solve the problem," Mrs. Watkins explained.

"I'll take care of him," Harriet promised. "Thank you for caring enough to bring him in. You did the right thing."

When Mr. Watkins reached into his back pocket and pulled out his wallet, Harriet stopped him. "There's no charge. Thanks again for bringing the cat to me."

"All right then," Mr. Watkins said. "Good day to you, Doctor, and to you, Vicar."

As soon as the couple left and were out of earshot, Will took the box from Harriet. "That was generous of you. Why didn't you take their money?"

"I don't want to discourage people from rescuing wounded animals, and I figure they're much more likely to bring them to me if they know they won't be stuck with a big vet bill. I'd rather let word get around that, just like Old Doc Bailey, the new Doc Bailey cares for strays free of charge."

Will smiled at her. "I'd say you're taking the parable of the great banquet to heart," he said. "I think it could apply to all God's creatures in the animal kingdom as well as to people."

Harriet smiled back at him as her heart warmed at his kind words. For Will to think that about her, well, it felt pretty wonderful.

CHAPTER TWELVE

With special soap and warm water, Harriet went to work bathing the squirming cat. Will held him firmly but gently. Harriet observed him with approval. Warmth spread through her as she watched his natural kindness come out for this stray cat. Not that his behavior surprised her. He'd once brought her an orphaned baby deer. He truly had a heart for every creature. When she stopped to consider the matter, she realized they had a lot in common.

"I'm so glad the Watkinses found you," Will murmured to the cat. "You're being such a brave boy."

Harriet beamed and sent up a prayer of gratitude for the same thing.

Charlie moseyed into the room to see what was going on followed by Maxwell, who greeted them with an enthusiastic wag of his tail. However, the smell the cat gave off was so strong that both clinic animals quickly left.

After she got him cleaned up, Harriet placed the cat gently into an empty cage. "He'll be asleep in no time. He must be exhausted from his ordeal. I'll let him be while I try to decide what to do with him. I'll also need to watch him for signs of gasoline poisoning." She washed her hands at the sink. Will did too.

"Do you keep a list of people who have mentioned an interest in adopting animals?" Will asked. "Or are you thinking about keeping him for yourself?"

Harriet smiled. "There's no way I can keep him. Charlie wouldn't approve. She's fine with the cats who are patients because she knows they're here temporarily, but I don't think she'd welcome a permanent addition, even one as sweet and handsome as this. I'll have to figure out something else for him. And I don't keep the kind of list you brought up, but maybe I should start."

"It appears that veterinarians don't really get a Sabbath, do they?" Will gave her a gentle smile.

"Not when there's an emergency." She sighed. "I'm pretty tired myself. Last week was particularly busy."

"How so?" Will asked. "I mean, besides your efforts to locate Gwen's lost dog."

"On Monday I had two sick-cow calls." She rattled off the list of tasks she'd performed to diagnose the cows and get them on the road to recovery. Both processes had lasted a few days. "Then there was an injured horse, a golden retriever who needed help delivering ten puppies, an abandoned rabbit who was rehomed, a goat who swallowed a rubber ball, a potbellied pig who needed her hooves trimmed, and a few others that escape me right now. Plus, of course, the usual annual checkups and vaccinations."

"That is a lot," Will said, his hazel eyes wide. "I had no idea you were so busy."

Chuckling, Harriet said, "As busy as a minister with his pastoral duties, I daresay. And speaking of pastoral duties—not that I need to add to them—but do you think you would have time to call on Gwen this week to offer her a word of encouragement? She's so distressed about this whole thing, which is understandable. Maybe you could pray with her and ease some of her anxiety."

"I can do that," Will said. "It's thoughtful of you to think of her."

"Thank you for agreeing, and for your help today," Harriet said. "And now I need a cup of tea and a slice of Aunt Jinny's chocolate cake. How about you?"

"That sounds great."

As he followed her from the surgery into the reception area, he paused to examine the old dog collar along with the medal on the corner of Polly's desk. "These are interesting. Surely they don't belong to one of your patients, do they?"

"No," Harriet said. "That's a Dickin Medal awarded to a dog named Rip shortly after World War II. The collar belonged to him as well."

Will nodded. "I've heard of the Dickin Medal. I saw a video a few months ago about a dog trained to sniff out electronic devices and drugs in a military camp in Afghanistan. It was a kind of an experiment—and it was very successful. The dog saved countless lives by foiling communications and preventing both insider and intruder attacks. He received the Dickin Medal just a couple of years ago."

"That's fascinating," Harriet said. "It's amazing how brave and intelligent these animals are and how many lives they've saved—and continue to save."

"So how did you come by these? Did you find them in your grandfather's belongings?"

"Actually, Van discovered them last week in the lost and found at the station. He brought them to me thinking I might know who they belonged to. I don't, but I'm trying to figure it out."

"Any clues so far?" Will asked.

"We think they might have been buried somewhere. You can see the dirt in the cracks in the leather and caked around some of the letters in the medal."

"Doesn't Van know who put them in the lost and found?" Will gave her a puzzled frown.

"He didn't see who did it," Harriet said.

"And I guess there's no way of knowing how long they might have been buried or even how long ago the person dug them up."

"Nope. Aunt Jinny and I have been racking our brains trying to figure it out. Do you know of a family in the village that might have had a dog named Rip back in the day?"

With a rueful smile, Will replied, "I haven't a clue. These pre-date my time here by decades."

Feeling her face get hot, Harriet corrected herself. "I meant have you heard of anyone still living here who might be descendants of Rip's owner? Grandchildren or great-grandchildren, perhaps, who still talk about their ancestor's remarkable dog?"

"Not off the top of my head." Will returned the items to the desk and opened the door for her. As they made their way back to Aunt Jinny's cottage, he said, "I could poke around in the old church records. I have several journals kept by previous pastors who served in 1916, during the Great War, as they called it. They aren't very detailed entries, and most are not especially exciting—more like a ship captain's log, making note of deaths, burials, weddings, things like that. I did see one entry regarding the women who were featured at the kissing booth at the church fete in 1942. Gave me a chuckle. We don't have kissing booths at the fete these days."

"That's interesting," Harriet said. "I really would appreciate it if you could check those records. I've promised myself to do what I can to see that the collar and medal are returned to whatever family they belong to, if at all possible."

"There's bound to be a fascinating story behind them," Will said. "Maybe you could check the newspaper archives too. I imagine that if a White Church Bay dog earned such an honor, it would be mentioned by the local press."

"Good idea."

Aunt Jinny welcomed them into her cottage and served the promised cake. Once she had their tea poured and everyone was settled, she wanted to hear all about the cat's condition.

Jane had taken her leave, so once Harriet had filled her aunt in about the cat, she felt more comfortable asking for Will's opinion regarding the strange note that Gwen had received about Petey. "On the one hand, I think it was rather a kind gesture, acknowledging Gwen's worry and assuring her that Petey would be returned. On the other hand, I'm concerned that the wording wasn't as clear as it should be. It didn't say Petey would be back in time for the London dog show. It didn't even say he would be returned unharmed, although the tone of the note did lead me to believe the writer wouldn't hurt him."

Will took a sip of tea, plainly gathering his thoughts. "The most interesting thing, of course, is what we mentioned earlier. Why did the dognapper send the note in the first place? Who's ever heard of an abduction with no ransom demanded?"

Aunt Jinny answered first. "I don't know what to think. The whole affair is bizarre."

"The only thing I can come up with is that a competitor wants to keep Gwen's dog out of the London show," Harriet said. "It's the only motive that makes sense, which is why I keep coming back to it." She savored another bite of cake. "Will, is Alistair's allergy really as serious as you say?"

Will nodded. "He told me so himself some time ago. I have no reason to believe he would lie to me about a thing like that."

"Very unlikely," Aunt Jinny agreed.

Harriet chewed the inside of her lip. Alistair Marling was an unlikely culprit, it was true. Still, she felt somewhat obligated to ask him about his whereabouts on the night in question. She needed to cover all the bases, right? But how she could do that without insulting the man was the problem. What if he accused her of slander? There could be legal complications. She hoped Jane wasn't running around the village telling people she'd seen Alistair with the missing dog. There could be negative consequences from that too.

But someone should talk with him—just to be sure.

Harriet was still mulling over the problem on Monday morning when Polly arrived at the clinic. Harriet asked her to put away the supplies that she'd purchased at the Pet Pangaea and then left for the Bender farm to see another sick cow. She also gave Polly specific instructions regarding the recovering cat. She'd dubbed him Smoky because of his gray fur.

"Are you keeping him?" Polly had asked, peering at the yawning cat in the cage. He was coming along nicely and showing no signs of having ingested the gasoline from his fur.

"Hopefully not. I need to find a good home for him though," Harriet told her. "Did you have a nice weekend?"

"Brilliant," Polly said with a grin. "And you?"

"I spent most of it investigating Petey's abduction."

Polly raised an inquiring eyebrow. "No luck, I take it?"

Harriet shook her head. "No luck. No clues. Nothing."

Polly put a comforting hand on her arm. "You'll get it worked out. You always do."

"I hope you're right." Harriet was beginning to lose faith in herself.

It was nearly lunchtime when she finished up at the Bender farm and returned to the clinic. Polly had left a note that she'd gone to lunch with a friend and would return shortly. After washing up and changing clothes, Harriet decided to drive to the village for lunch.

But first, she'd visit Alistair Marling. She wouldn't get a moment's peace until she did. She hadn't worked out what she'd say, but she wanted to watch his expression and observe his body language. All the way there, she prayed for the right words.

The crisp autumn sea air eased her trepidation as she parked near Alistair's office a short while later. It was a small establishment sandwiched between a yarn shop and a pawnshop. The sign for Marling Insurance was large, with bold letters that could be read far down the busy street.

A bell tinkled overhead when she entered. The front desk was empty, so Harriet assumed the secretary was out to lunch.

Alistair emerged from the back office to greet her with a bright smile. "Dr. Bailey, good afternoon." He reached out to shake her hand. His was large and warm, his handshake firm. He wore dark gray slacks and a cream-colored shirt with a plaid tie. His shoes had been polished to a high sheen. His brown eyes met her gaze with frankness. "A beautiful day, wouldn't you say?"

Harriet stared up at him. He was indeed tall. She squared her shoulders and took a deep breath. "Before you get your hopes up that I've come to ask about an insurance policy, I need to tell you that I'm here on a different matter altogether."

His face remained pleasantly neutral, the professional smile firmly in place. If her announcement caught him by surprise, he certainly didn't let on. "Then you'd better come in and have a seat."

Harriet sat down in the armchair he indicated beside his massive desk. "I know you're a busy man, and I won't take up much of your time. I'm hoping you'd be willing to tell me where you were on Thursday night between six thirty and eight thirty."

He raised a thin eyebrow. "Now I really am curious. But I can tell you I was dining at home during that time." He reached for a burgundy appointment book, opened it, and flipped a page or two. "I had no appointments that evening. As I recall, it rained quite heavily. Yes, I stayed in with my wife. We watched a BBC mystery on the telly." Lacing his fingers and resting his hands on his desk, Alistair asked, "Do you mind telling me why you want to know?"

Harriet gave him a small smile, trying to ignore a slight surge of dread. She truly didn't want to offend the man. "Gwen Higginbottom's Scottish terrier went missing that evening. Someone thought they saw you on the street at that time. If you were indeed out and about then, did you happen to see the dog running down the sidewalk or cowering underneath the eaves of a shop or home? We're hunting for any leads we can find, hoping to locate the dog."

Alistair blinked but exhibited no sign of guilt or embarrassment. "Someone is mistaken, I must say."

Harriet silently hoped he wouldn't ask who that someone was.

"As I said, I was not out and about," Alistair assured her. "I have, however, heard about the missing dog. My secretary saw a flyer posted somewhere. I do hope Miss Higginbottom will find her dog soon."

"We all do. Petey is supposed to compete in the London dog show at the end of the month, and we're anxious to find him," Harriet told him.

"Surely Rand Cromwell has been notified," Alistair said.

"Yes, and the police too. Everyone is on the lookout."

"I suppose dogs run away from time to time. Hers might have been frightened by the thunder and lightning." Alistair stroked his chin. "I don't know much about dogs, since I've never had one, but I suppose he'll return home sooner or later."

"I heard you are allergic to dogs," Harriet said carefully.

"You heard correctly. Dogs, cats, hamsters, rabbits—anything with fur." He shuddered. "Having asthma complicates things too, so I've never owned a pet and have to be careful. My wife would love to have a dog, but my allergies prevent it. I get allergy shots, so if I had a reaction, hopefully it wouldn't be as severe as it could be, but I'm not willing to take chances."

Harriet smothered a sigh of relief and rose. The conversation had not been nearly as prickly as she'd feared. Now she needed to make her escape before the man pitched a policy her way. Jane may have seen a tall man carrying Petey away, but Harriet felt confident that man wasn't Alistair Marling.

"Thank you for your time," Harriet said. "If you do catch sight of Petey, please call me or the police station or the dogcatcher. We're keen to recover the dog as soon as possible."

Alistair rose as well. "Certainly. Maybe you can stop by again. Please keep me in mind for any of your insurance coverage needs."

"I will. Thank you." Harriet made good her escape.

On the positive side, she was confident she'd eliminated Alistair as a suspect. On the negative side, that meant she still had no idea where Petey could possibly be.

London
May 1941

Dear Malcolm,

Your letter arrived by post yesterday. You asked if the bombing is still as heavy as before. Luckily, it's not. Things seem to be slowing down, at least here in London. I reckon Hitler has decided to spread his bombers to terrify the rest of jolly old England. Liverpool got it yesterday, and the Surrey docks the day before.

You can hear the drone of the planes from quite a distance. Rip sure can. He'll growl and get all fidgety. When the bombs start falling, they make a whooshing sound, sort of like a crowd cheering at a football match rather than that whistling noise they use in the films. The noise is deafening. The ground shakes too. I think the daytime bombing is more demoralizing because the blue sky gets clouded with smoke from all the fires. Of course, the nighttime bombings are perhaps more frightening because you feel more vulnerable in the dark. So I can't say I prefer one or the other. I'd prefer neither, of course, but who knows when that will happen? Or if it ever will?

Hearing the long wail from the warning siren still gives me the same cold knot of fear in the pit of my stomach. I thought I would get used to it, but I begin to suspect that will never happen either.

I'll have to hand it to Rip. He doesn't know what's going on, not really. He's only a dog, after all. But despite the noise of the bombs and fire engine bells and antiaircraft guns, he keeps his head and goes about his business. And I try to take my cue from him.

Recently, I met a young copper by the name of Irwin. He's new on the beat. He comes along now on our rounds to keep an eye on those who are light-fingered, so to speak. Can you believe it? There are actually people who steal from the unfortunates who have lost their homes to the bombs and gone to live elsewhere. If Irwin catches anyone in the act, he hauls them off to the nick. It's a shame that looters are taking advantage of people's troubles and stealing their few remaining belongings.

Irwin told us that during the blitz last year, some thieves would kit themselves out with an ARP warden's helmet and armband and smash their way into shops when no one was looking. Some of the villains used vehicles disguised as ambulances for their getaways. Irwin says that with so many young men away to war, the police force has been weakened. Gangs are taking advantage of the situation. They even yank brooches and rings and watches off corpses in the rubble. I am sickened by the very idea.

Irwin's father is an engine driver on the railway. He spends most of his time transporting the armed forces to and from London. Irwin asked about my missing fingers, but hardly anyone notices them at this point. Some men who are young enough to wear the uniform are harassed by folks when they are seen about town, so I let people think I lost my fingers on the battlefield rather than in a farming accident. We should not be too quick to judge. Some guys have unseen ailments that keep them from joining the army. Most of them serve in other ways.

The ARP still plays a key role in managing the response to the raids. We issue gas masks in case of attacks from the air. We inspect shelters and make sure blackout rules are followed. When the sirens sound, we help those fleeing to safety and patrol the streets. We put ourselves at risk, but there's a war on. We do what we must do. And we're getting plenty of help from others, so don't worry about that. The Auxiliary Fire Service is part of the ARP. They tackle the blazes that result from the bombings. And we've got all sorts of medical services and volunteers like the Home Guard and even the Scouts.

By the way, Irwin has a sister named Cecily, who owns a café nearby. We had lunch there the other day. The Singing Canary, it's called. Everything inside is a sunny yellow. Real cheerful with floral oilcloth on the tables and bright touches everywhere. The windows are patched with plywood. Cecily says she's not going to replace the shattered glass until Hitler finds something else to do besides bomb the stuffing out of us.

Did I tell you that at one time a gent with the War Ministry suggested folks put strips of brown paper over the windows to keep them from breaking? It always did seem barmy to me to think that paper would prevent glass from shattering when the bombs fell.

Cecily sets a fine table. We had pork chops, boiled potatoes, and an apple pudding for a bit of sweet. The three of us got to talking about the possibility of invasion. Irwin says that if Hitler can drop bombs, he can drop soldiers too. I do worry about that.

Before I left, Irwin told Cecily about Rip and what a fine member of the recovery team he is. You know what she did? She went right back into her kitchen and returned with a pork chop for old Rip. Cecily is a real sport, she is. You can bet Rip appreciated the treat, and he's earned every bit of it. He's now located more than seventy-five trapped souls. We rescued them, but he found them.

Stay calm and carry on!

Brad

CHAPTER THIRTEEN

The tantalizing aromas wafting from the White Hart tempted Harriet inside. Noting that the special of the day was Dover sole with scalloped potatoes, she heard her stomach rumble. She hadn't realized just how hungry she was. Now that the tourist season was over, she could enjoy lunch without having to wait half an hour or more for a table.

When she noticed Doreen Danby sitting at a table for two by the window, she made her way over in that direction. "Mind a little company?"

Doreen glanced up and paused from forking a piece of ham into her mouth. Her face beaming with pleasure, she exclaimed, "Harriet, how lovely. Please join me."

Harriet pulled out the chair across from Doreen's, sat down, and hung her shoulder bag on the back of the chair. When the waitress came over, Harriet ordered the special. "I love the food here," she told her friend.

"Me too," Doreen replied. "I don't often have an opportunity to eat out like this, but Ella had a dentist appointment this morning. After I took her back to the school, I decided I deserved a little treat."

Harriet looked at Doreen's plate loaded with ham, mashed potatoes, and sautéed vegetables and said, "It looks like you got it."

"It's so nice to eat someone else's cooking. Even toast with Bovril tastes better when someone else makes it."

Harriet laughed and wrinkled her nose. She had not yet acquired a taste for the salty meat spread that many of her British friends enjoyed. She doubted she ever would.

Doreen went on. "I may drop by the bakery on my way home and pick up some scones."

"Why?" Harriet asked. "You make the best scones around. I doubt you'll find anything at the bakery better than your own."

"Thank you for that, but like I said, it's a pleasure to eat food that someone else has made."

Considering her own enjoyment of Aunt Jinny's cooking, Harriet couldn't argue with that. She changed the subject instead. "Want a cat?"

"No!" Doreen replied emphatically. "Why? Are you giving Charlie away?"

"Never." Harriet explained about Smoky and his horrible ordeal.

The waitress arrived and set a steaming plate in front of Harriet.

After Harriet had scooped up a forkful of creamy potatoes, she said, "I'd really like to find a good home for the cat."

"You will." Doreen cast a quick glance over her shoulder, as if making sure they wouldn't be overheard, then said, "By the way, did you visit the Decker place over the weekend? Did you ask Van to go with you?"

"Yes, he and I went out there first thing Saturday morning."

Doreen leaned in. "What happened?"

Harriet shared the details of their visit. "At one point I thought Rupert was going to lose his temper with us, but he didn't. I tried to let Van do the talking."

"Was Clarence there?"

"He was, and he struck me as a gentle soul. I don't believe he'd hurt Petey even if he and his father did abduct the dog. Which they didn't. They both have alibis."

Doreen raised an eyebrow. However, she didn't pry for details. Instead, she asked, "Did Rupert invite you inside?"

"No," Harriet replied. "I was sort of hoping he would. I thought I might catch a glimpse of some yellow rain gear hanging on a peg somewhere, but he kept us out in the yard. Not a very hospitable person, is he?"

"Not at all. Did Clarence show you his collection of rescued animals?"

"He didn't, and I would really have loved to see them," Harriet said. "Call it professional curiosity. And I think he would have liked to show me, but it didn't seem like the right time to ask. Rupert was already unhappy with our presence."

"Yes," Doreen said, "I can imagine him glaring at you both. He doesn't like snoops. Or doctors. Or constables. But Clarence isn't painted with the same brush as his father."

"You believe he can be trusted with animals?" Harriet tipped her head.

"Absolutely," Doreen replied. "Like I said before, he's fonder of animals than people. He's good with them too—animals, I mean."

"Hmm, then I may ask him to take Smoky."

"You can trust Clarence to care for him," Doreen assured her.

As Harriet applied herself to her meal, a sudden thought occurred to her. "Does Rupert Decker resent his son's little zoo? I'm sure it costs quite a bit to feed all those animals, not to mention the cost of building and repairing the pens and cages."

Doreen shrugged. "As far as I know, he doesn't make a fuss about that sort of thing, and Clarence keeps collecting animals from hither and yon."

"Perhaps Rupert Decker is more like his son than we realize," Harriet mused. "Fonder of animals than his fellow man. Ivanhoe is clearly well cared for and well trained, and the man seems fond of his dog. I can't fault him there."

She took the last delicious bite of fish while considering taking Smoky to the Decker place and asking Clarence to care for him. Maybe she could see his collection then. She'd have to plan on going out there some weekday when Rupert was away on a job. She didn't relish the idea of meeting him again anytime soon, no matter how kind a pet owner he might be.

"Any new developments besides crossing the Deckers off the suspect list?" Doreen inquired, interrupting Harriet's reverie.

"One. Gwen received a note in the post, unsigned and scribbled in a rather childish scrawl. It said Petey would be returned soon."

Doreen sat bolt upright in her chair. "The plot thickens. Was it a ransom note demanding money for the dog's return?"

Harriet shook her head. "It actually told her not to worry and seemed to indicate that whoever took Petey means to return him."

Doreen gaped at her. "Really? That's not exactly what I expected."

"We're all befuddled. Gwen doesn't know what to think, and I don't know what to do next."

Tamzin Pickers entered the inn's dining room. She was fashionably dressed in black jeans and a red wool blazer, and she went to the counter to pick up a to-go box. She left again without glancing around the restaurant.

Doreen grabbed Harriet's attention again when she said, "Hey, share an apple crisp with me?"

Harriet smiled. "Sure, if we can get it with warm custard sauce." It was one of the pleasures Harriet had come to appreciate now that she'd moved to England—all the varieties of cream, such as creamy custards, Devonshire cream, clotted cream, and crème fraîche. Thick, rich, and delicious.

"Is there any other way to order it?" Doreen waved her hand in the air to attract their waitress. Over dessert and coffee, they discussed Petey's abduction and possible reasons why anyone would send such a note to Gwen.

"Just from that message, you can definitely strike Rupert Decker from your list of possible suspects, even if he didn't have an alibi," Doreen said, licking custard from the back of her spoon. "I can't imagine him ever using the word *please*. His manners are sorely lacking." She took a bite of apple crisp, closed her eyes, and hummed in appreciation.

Once again, Harriet contemplated the note Gwen had received. It had a feminine ring to it—the writer used the words *sweet* and *handsome*. The penmanship had appeared immature, either a young person's hand or that of someone purposefully disguising his handwriting. And what did such a note have to do with a tall man dashing through the rain with Petey under one arm?

"I wish this mystery was already solved," Harriet said finally.

Doreen nodded, her mouth full of custard and fruit. After swallowing and dabbing her mouth with her napkin, she asked, "What about the other mystery, the one with the dog collar and medal? Have you discovered anything new?"

"We have," Harriet said. "Aunt Jinny and I did some research online and discovered that the medallion is a Dickin Medal, given by the PDSA, or People's Dispensary for Sick Animals. It was first awarded to animals for their courage in World War II, but they've given the medal to animals from World War I, Korea, and more recent conflicts."

"Do they honor only British animals?" Doreen asked.

"No. I read they gave the medal to a dog who represented all the ones who assisted rescue workers after the September 11 attacks in New York City. There were dogs honored who led people to safety from the seventieth story of one of the World Trade Center buildings."

"So were you able to find any information about the medal Van gave you?"

"Oh, Doreen, it's so amazing. A dog named Rip received the award in 1945 for his efforts as a search and rescue dog during the war. In one year alone, he saved over a hundred victims of air raids."

"Now isn't that something?" Doreen exclaimed, obviously impressed. "I don't recall anyone here with a dog who was famous for something like that. But then, 1945 is way before my time."

"Still, you'd think the family would boast about it, wouldn't you?" Harriet asked. "Even though it happened ages ago?"

"Maybe, maybe not. Time passes. People move away. Family legends are lost."

"True, but I feel certain that with a little digging, I'll be able to locate a family member related to the man or woman who used to own Rip," Harriet insisted. "Surely someone remembers back in the day when their grandfather or great-grandfather had a dog honored for gallantry. I'm not ready to give up yet."

"I wish you luck." Doreen put down her fork.

"I'm going to keep hunting until I find more information. There's a photo of Rip on the PDSA website. It looks like he's smiling. I think he must have been quite a character. I liked the looks of him." Harriet grinned.

Doreen chuckled. "You like the looks of most dogs. That's why you're a good vet." With a shrug she added, "If there's anything I can do, say the word. Happy to help when I can."

Harriet's phone pinged. She reached into her purse and discovered a text from Polly.

CAN YOU COME BACK ASAP? INJURED TURTLE.

Harriet texted that she was on her way. "Sorry to cut this short, Doreen, but duty calls. I have a patient waiting at the clinic." She dug in her wallet for the necessary cash to pay her tab.

"Nothing too serious, I hope."

"Nothing I can't handle," Harriet assured her, setting the money on the table.

On the way to the clinic she tried to force thoughts of Petey to the back of her mind. Her concern for the little terrier was taking up a lot of time and effort, and her other patients deserved her attention as well.

She walked into the exam room and was soon absorbed in examining a turtle with a minor shell infection. She praised the worried owner for noticing and bringing in his pet before the infection was too bad and assured him that all would soon be well. After treating the turtle and saying goodbye to the relieved pet owner,

Harriet returned a few phone calls and checked on Smoky, who was still doing well.

"How about a cuppa?" Polly asked. "It's been a busy afternoon, with phone calls mostly. I've lined up a few appointments for you this week."

"I would love a cup of tea." Harriet took a deep breath as she plunked down in a chair near Polly's desk. She closed her eyes for a moment and tried not to think of anything at all. Her brain needed a rest.

But no sooner had Polly returned with a mug of hot tea than Harriet's cell phone rang. Reaching for it, she was mildly surprised to see Will's name appear on the screen.

"Am I interrupting anything?" he asked. His tone sounded light and playful. *Not an emergency then.*

Harriet sighed in relief. "I was sitting down to enjoy a break with Polly." She glanced at her assistant, mouthed the word *short-bread*, and pointed in the direction of the kitchen.

Polly grinned, retreating immediately to fetch the cookies.

In a cheerful voice, Harriet asked, "What can I do for you?"

"Actually, Harriet, it's what I can do for you. I've discovered the name of the lucky man who once owned Rip, the gallant rescue dog."

CHAPTER FOURTEEN

Twenty minutes later, Harriet left the clinic in Polly's capable hands and took off for the rectory. She found Will waiting for her at the front door, his hands in his pockets and his face shining with eagerness and self-satisfaction. "I can't believe I found it so quickly," he said, ushering her inside out of the blustery weather.

Will led her through the foyer and past the parlor to his study—a masculine room, all aged leather and mahogany wood. He invited her to sit in a large black leather chair in front of his desk. The massive chair creaked when she lowered herself into it. It surely dated to Victorian times, Harriet decided, noting how her feet barely touched the floor when she sat all the way back.

"How about some tea or coffee?" Will suggested. "There's hot cider too, I think. Something to take the chill off?"

"No thanks," Harriet said, glancing around the study and wondering how many previous pastors had called this room their own.

Will smiled, his eyes gleaming with good humor. He sat down in his desk chair. "All right, I can see you're eager to learn what I've discovered."

Chuckling, Harriet asked, "Is it that obvious?"

"I'm surprised you haven't started going through my desk already," he teased.

Harriet couldn't deny it. "I'm sorry. I'm hoping your discovery will move this mystery forward and not result in another dead end. I'm making no headway in figuring out where Petey is or how to get him back, so it would be a blessing to find out some details about Rip and his owner, making progress in one area at least."

"I understand that," he said, his tone becoming gentler. "I started with the pastors' journals dating back to 1945, because you said that's when Rip received his medal. That date proved to be quite helpful in narrowing my search." He pushed what appeared to be a large ledger across the desk toward her. It was covered with faded blue cloth that was slightly frayed around the edges, and was open to a few pages from the end. "There's his name. Bradley Welks," Will announced. "That's the man who owned Rip." He pointed to a name in the center of the lefthand side of the page.

Harriet immediately felt an uptick in her pulse as she read the name and the entry about him. The pastor at the time made a note that Bradley Welks had joined the church and that his dog Rip was to receive a prestigious Dickin Medal from the Lord Mayor of London. Several of Bradley's kinsmen were to travel to attend the ceremony.

Harriet laughed with delight. She could almost sense the pride with which the long-ago minister had made the notation. "It says here the church fete committee asked Bradley Welks and Rip to open the fundraiser. What an honor. They became local celebrities, didn't they?"

"Indeed," Will answered.

The church fete in the summer was a big deal in the village. Nearly all the residents participated, and tourists seemed to enjoy it too.

"Then surely there would have been an article about Rip in the local paper," Harriet went on.

"Yes, I feel certain there must have been," Will agreed. "Probably on the society page. And who knows? Maybe something on the front page about Rip receiving the medal. After all, it's not every day a dog receives such an honor from the Lord Mayor of London."

"Bradley Welks." Harriet repeated the name. "It doesn't ring a bell. I don't think I know anyone with that surname. Do you?"

Will shook his head. "Not that I can recall. But the notation says he had local kinsmen of some sort. Some of them may still be living in town."

"Any idea who they might be?"

"It doesn't say here. But I might have an idea," Will said. "There are no further mentions of Bradley Welks until his funeral. So I looked through the official church records of births, marriages, and deaths, and found out he died in November 1963."

"Wow, you were thorough," Harriet said, impressed.

"This is important." Will reached for another open ledger and pushed it across the desk toward Harriet. "The notation halfway down the page shows that the pastor at the time visited Bradley Welks in the hospital. He was quite ill with pneumonia. Apparently, he died shortly afterward and was buried in the cemetery here. A man named Malcolm Danby paid for the funeral services."

Harriet jolted upright. "Did you say Danby?" Surely there was some relation to Doreen's husband, Tom. "Could you make a photocopy of this page and the one about Bradley and Rip? I'd really appreciate it."

"Not a problem." Will stood and carried one of the books to a copier on the other side of the room. "Photocopying is one of my superpowers. You can't imagine how often I'm asked to make copies of church records for people tracing their genealogy or searching for marriage and death dates."

While he went about his task, Harriet made plans to speak with Doreen as soon as possible about the link between Tom's family and Bradley Welks. Doreen must be unfamiliar with the connection, because she hadn't recognized the name of the dog when Harriet mentioned it to her over lunch.

"I bet the Malcolm Danby mentioned in the church records is some sort of relation to Tom Danby." Harriet spoke her thoughts out loud as Will handed her the copies.

"Could be," he agreed.

Harriet glanced at her watch. It was getting late in the day, and the sun would be setting soon. She rose and tucked the pages into her bag. "Do you think I could see Bradley Welks's grave before I go?"

"Of course. I have a vague idea where it might be located in the cemetery," Will said. "Follow me." He took his jacket from a peg on the back of the door and led the way to the churchyard.

Harriet saw at once that many of the older gravestones dated to the 1800s, and she guessed that some were even more ancient than that, but their writing had been worn away by time and the elements. She recognized several familiar surnames. Many of her neighbors had family ties to the church that stretched back over generations.

Noticing again the long strip of dark, overturned earth near the wall of the church building, she asked, "What are you planting?"

Will followed her gaze. "The sexton planted daffodils along the wall there as part of a new flower bed. They'll make for a cheerful splash of color come spring."

"I love daffodils," Harriet said with a smile.

"They're always a nice change from the cold dullness of winter," Will agreed. He pointed. "Over there."

Despite the late afternoon shadows, Harriet could read *Bradley Josiah Welks* engraved on the simple stone. The name was followed by *1920–1963* and the words *Leaning on the Everlasting Arms.*

Harriet felt a twinge of sorrow. Bradley had been a decade older than she was when he succumbed to pneumonia. "He was so young."

Will nodded. "Too young. He might have been a soldier who never recovered his strength after the war. Besides, people used to die from pneumonia quite a lot in those days."

"According to Aunt Jinny, pneumonia is still a rather common cause of death," Harriet said. "I wonder if Bradley Welks was a soldier."

"I don't know, but now that you have his full name and the dates of his birth and death, you might be able to do some online research and discover that for yourself."

Harriet nodded. She slowly knelt beside the grave to examine the grass growing on it. "It doesn't look disturbed at all."

"Did you expect it would be?" Will asked.

Rising again, she said, "Do you remember how the dog collar and medal were caked with dirt? The logical conclusion is that they were buried at some point. If so, they probably weren't buried in Bradley Welks's grave."

"Surely those things would have been buried with the dog," Will said.

"Probably," Harriet agreed. "Does that mean someone dug up Rip's grave? There aren't any animals buried here in the churchyard, are there?"

Will seemed surprised by the question. "I don't believe so."

"Then where did the collar and medal come from? And who left them in the lost and found at the police station?" Harriet asked.

Will shrugged. "Those are very good questions for which I have no answers."

CHAPTER FIFTEEN

When Harriet returned to the clinic, Polly was already gone for the day. She'd left a note that she'd run to Pet Pangaea to pick up an order. She'd also left a small stack of pink phone slips. A quick perusal of the messages revealed that none were emergencies. Given the hour, Harriet decided she would return the calls in the morning.

As she finished preparing for the following day at the clinic, Aunt Jinny popped her head through the door. "Want to come over for soup and a cheese toastie? I've got a block of that Irish cheddar you like."

"Sounds good," Harriet said, suddenly hungry. "While we eat, I can tell you what I learned about Bradley Welks."

"And who might he be?" her aunt asked as she bent down to give Maxwell a scratch behind his ear. Charlie had sauntered in to see who had arrived, no doubt wondering what all the fuss was about.

"Bradley Welks was the proud owner of Rip, the gallant search and rescue dog we've been reading about," Harriet said, beaming. It felt good to make progress along those lines, especially since her efforts to locate Petey had not yet come to fruition.

Aunt Jinny's face lit up. "That's wonderful! We're learning a little more each day, it seems. Sooner or later, we'll have the whole story. I feel certain of it. How did you come to find this out?"

"Will discovered a few pertinent facts in some local church records," Harriet said. "Bradley and Rip even opened the church fete one summer."

"That's quite an honor for a local hero. I want to hear all about it while we eat. Maxwell can come along if he wants to."

As Harriet scooped up her purse and cell phone, Maxwell wagged his tail and followed Aunt Jinny through the door into the evening gloom. The wind had picked up, and the temperature had dropped. Harriet pulled her jacket collar up around her throat. Soon it would be heavy-coat weather. Sweaters and jackets wouldn't be enough to keep out the chill.

As they strode up the narrow path leading to Aunt Jinny's cottage, which glowed invitingly from the lamplight inside, a vehicle's headlights pierced the darkness behind them. Harriet turned, wondering who was dropping in at this hour. She quickly recognized Polly's car and felt a twinge of anxiety. Had she forgotten something at her desk, or was something wrong?

"Wait a minute. It's Polly," she said to her aunt.

Polly hopped out of the car and dashed toward her with a stack of cardboard pet carriers in her arms—the kind Harriet occasionally gave clients to transport their sedated pets safely home in.

"Polly, you didn't need to bring those over here now," Harriet told her. "You could have waited until tomorrow."

"I didn't come just to deliver these. I have something to tell you, and it might be important," Polly gushed breathlessly. Even in the dark, Harriet could see that her friend's expression held a combination of concern and excitement.

Maxwell waddled to Polly, wagging his tail vigorously. Polly was one of his favorite humans, and he never failed to let her know it.

Aunt Jinny joined them in the middle of the path. "Is everything all right?"

"I overheard something at Pet Pangaea just now," Polly explained. "It might have something to do with Petey."

"Let's not stand out here in the cold," Aunt Jinny said. "We'll catch a chill. Come into the house."

Polly obediently fell in behind her, and Harriet brought up the rear. She wondered what was so important that Polly would drive out here with such a sense of urgency.

Inside her aunt's cozy English countryside kitchen, Harriet caught the aroma of Aunt Jinny's hearty vegetable soup simmering on the stove. Her stomach growled. She must be hungrier than she'd realized.

"Put those over there, Polly." Aunt Jinny indicated the cardboard carriers. "Have a seat and tell us what's happened while I make the sandwiches."

Polly did as she was told, plopping down in a kitchen chair. She crossed her arms and leaned them on the table. "To be clear, I don't want to get anyone in trouble. But it could be important, and the incident struck me as a bit odd, so I thought you should know about it, Harriet."

Harriet raised her eyebrows. "Okay, tell me."

"I went to Pet Pangaea to pick up the carriers you ordered." Polly tilted her head toward the counter where she'd piled them. "Tamzin was ringing up purchases for Mindy Milner, all sorts of dog supplies. Food, dog bowls, chews, a brush—the works."

"So?" Aunt Jinny asked.

Harriet felt confused too. "Who's Mindy Milner? Should I know her?"

"She's Mrs. Dalton's niece," Polly answered. "You treated Mrs. Dalton's Yorkie a while back, remember?"

"Sure, but what does that have to do with anything?"

"Mindy Milner doesn't own a dog. But she does have a tall husband. Quite tall, as a matter of fact. Wouldn't you say Tad Milner is tall?" Polly asked Aunt Jinny, who nodded in agreement as she worked on the grilled cheese.

Harriet shrugged. "So maybe they got a new dog. That would explain all the purchases."

Polly shook her head. "Tamzin asked if they'd bought or adopted a dog. Mindy said no, that she was buying everything for a friend. But what if she was lying? What if Tad is the tall man who kidnapped Petey, and Mindy bought the necessary supplies to care for him?"

"I would have thought they'd buy the necessary supplies *before* they snatched the dog," Aunt Jinny pointed out.

"I agree," Harriet put in. "It's been days now since Petey disappeared. He would have needed food and other things before now. Maybe she really did buy the supplies for a friend."

"Hey, someone took Petey," Polly said. "That's a fact, proven by the note Gwen got. Everyone you first suspected seems to have an alibi or at least a reason why it couldn't have been them. Now this woman who doesn't own a dog is buying dog supplies. She has a tall husband who may own yellow rain gear. Perhaps they're planning to take care of a dog—like, say, Petey—for some unknown length of time."

Harriet frowned dubiously. "How well do you know this Mindy person?"

"Not well at all. She's a friend of my mum's. But I know the Milners don't own a dog," Polly insisted.

Harriet wasn't sure what to say to that.

"I know how to settle this." Aunt Jinny reached for her cell phone and punched in a number. "Hello, Mrs. Dalton, it's Dr. Garrett. How are you this evening?"

Harriet listened with admiration while her aunt spoke to the woman on the phone, inquiring about her health and even asking about Winnie, the woman's cute little Yorkie. Soon she brought the questions around to Mindy and her husband, Tad. Although Harriet couldn't hear Mrs. Dalton's responses, she could make a few educated guesses based on Aunt Jinny's replies.

"I understand Mindy and her husband are getting a new puppy, and I wanted to remind you that my niece, Harriet, does puppy wellness appointments if they have any concerns," Aunt Jinny said cheerily. "Is it a Yorkie like your sweet Winnie? What's that? That's interesting. No, I totally understand. If I had a new white carpet, I certainly wouldn't want a puppy either. Right, or even an adult dog whose temperament I didn't know."

Aunt Jinny soon brought the conversation to a close, wished Mrs. Dalton a pleasant evening, and then ended the call, looking worried. "If Mindy Milner is getting a puppy, it's news to her aunt. She said Mindy and Tad just had their living room newly carpeted in a lovely shade of creamy white. It's highly unlikely that they're getting a dog."

"See?" Polly said. "I knew she wasn't buying those supplies for herself." She looked at them triumphantly.

But we don't know that for sure," Harriet protested. "She might have been telling the truth, that she was purchasing the pet supplies for a friend."

Polly sighed. "I know it's a long shot, but I so badly want to find Petey. I just think it's possible that the Milners took the dog and plan to return him later. Why they would do such a thing, I can't begin to guess. It struck me as odd, so I jumped on it. What are we going to do now?"

"Frankly, I don't know," Harriet admitted. "We've exhausted every idea I can come up with. All our other suspects have been crossed off the list." She sighed. "I feel as if we're never going to find Petey."

Aunt Jinny placed her hand on Harriet's shoulder. "We know you're worried, Harriet. You care about Petey. We all do. But we can't allow ourselves to get discouraged. Remember, God knows where that little dog is, and I trust soon we'll know too."

"You're absolutely right," Harriet said. She smiled at her aunt. "I'm starving," she announced. "I can't think clearly on an empty stomach, and I don't think anyone else can either. Polly, why don't you join us for soup and grilled cheese?"

"Mum's expecting me for dinner," Polly hedged.

"Call her and let her know you're dining here with us," Aunt Jinny suggested. "We have plenty."

"Besides," Harriet insisted, "I want to tell you both about Rip and Bradley Welks."

"Well, I can't miss that." Polly rose from her chair and left the kitchen to make the call.

Aunt Jinny finished preparing the food while Harriet set the table. Polly came back, and they sat down to eat. The food was delicious and the conversation lively. Harriet shared all she'd learned from Will about Bradley Welks and his dog Rip. "And to think, the man is buried in the church cemetery, right here in the village."

It was nearly nine o'clock when the impromptu dinner party broke up. Harriet's mood had lightened. And Polly had agreed to forget about the Milners and to concentrate instead on learning something about Rip and Bradley. "I'm going to ask Gran if she remembers anyone by that name. She'd have been a girl back then. She might remember a dog who'd won a medal for valor, right? I mean, it's so exciting," she said as she cleared dishes from the table.

"And did I mention that Bradley Welks was related to a Danby?" Harriet added.

"Danby?" Aunt Jinny repeated. "As in Tom and Doreen Danby?"

Harriet raised her eyebrows. "Could be. I'm really hoping so anyway. Will made photocopies of the journal entries for me. Someone named Malcolm Danby paid for Bradley's funeral. Will showed me the grave. He died of pneumonia in 1963. He was only in his forties."

Aunt Jinny tutted. "Pneumonia is no small matter, that's for sure."

As Polly crouched to give Maxwell one last back rub, Harriet asked her, "Would you mind keeping the information about the Milners to yourself? I don't want Jane and Gwen to hear about Mindy's purchases. They might consider the couple to be suspects in Petey's abduction and get carried away with their own sleuthing."

"Good idea," Polly said. "Their first hunches were way off the mark, weren't they?"

"Maybe our earnest young detective constable can make inquiries," Aunt Jinny suggested. "Van is officially working the case after all."

"And he's doing the best he can," Polly said. "I think he's as frustrated about it as we are."

"That wouldn't surprise me," Harriet said. "But we private citizens must tread lightly. There could be legal complications if people are publicly accused of stealing a dog. Defamation, slander, those sorts of things." She wasn't sure how such accusations might play out, but they had to be careful.

Harriet began to wonder about the toll the situation was taking on Petey. Friendly as he was, he must be as frightened and anxious as Gwen under the circumstances. Was he eating? Did he whine all day for his beloved owner?

The thought that someone outside the village might have stolen Petey caused a knot to twist in the pit of her stomach. If that was the case, they might never find him. Gwen would be caught somewhere between heartbreak and hope for the rest of her life.

London

August 1942

Dear Malcolm,

I'm so sorry to hear that German aeroplanes have found their way to Yorkshire. I hope the damage is not too considerable and that everyone in the village is all right. I thank the Lord that you all escaped any damage on the farm.

The city here is quite battered. It saddens me to see children playing in the piles of rubble, though it also keeps me from despair, reminding me that life continues in spite of the devastation. Yes, the London docks may be a wreck and that regal old cathedral in Coventry burned to the ground, but St. Paul's is still standing despite many nearby buildings being reduced to nothing. It's an inspiration to us all to see that cathedral framed by smoke and fire but still standing strong and defiant. There's a Civil Defense brigade responsible for its protection, and the St. Paul's Fire Watch is on alert round the clock. We all look forward to the day when the bells will ring out celebrating the end of the war. It can't be soon enough to suit me. In the meantime, we carry on because we must.

Earlier this week, a rocket landed in our sector, destroying several homes and damaging others. The gas line was compromised, so we hurried to get survivors out of the area as soon as possible. We rescued a woman named Mrs. Gridley and her two girls right away and thought we'd done our duty. But Rip thought otherwise. He scaled a ten-foot pile of debris, scrambling up to the top in no time. He barked at us and began digging. We've learned by now not to doubt him, so Garrick and I got to work at his side. The heavy-duty rescue team lent a hand.

Moments later, we heard the faint cries of a baby beneath our feet.

As you can imagine, we set to with a vengeance after that, determined to rescue the little mite. We found him and his mother trapped in one of those Morrison shelters. When we freed them from their prison of debris, the young mother was so grateful. She could hardly believe it when we told her that Rip was responsible for their rescue.

While a medical team lifted her and the baby onto a stretcher, Rip licked her hand, as if reassuring her everything was going to be okay. Isn't that something? He even licked the baby's face, which stopped the little tyke from crying. The mother burst into tears of relief. She couldn't stop thanking us all. A good night's work, I call it. Turns out her husband's away in the navy. Least we can do at home is take care of the families of those men fighting on our behalf.

We're all proud of Rip, I can tell you. He has the best ears, and there's no fooling his nose. He can smell survivors ten or twenty feet below the rubble. Amazing, isn't it? Old Rip just seems to shake off the fear of fire and smoke.

You remember I told you about Irwin, the young officer who started policing here a little more than a year ago. Irwin admires Rip something fierce. Declared the little dog goes where angels fear to tread and that the police would do well to take on some dogs to help fight crime and such. Irwin joked that when the war is over, he's going to look into hiring Rip onto the police force. But if Rip and I survive this war, we're coming home to White Church Bay—together. Yes sir, I'm bringing old Rip back with me. I call him old, but truth be told, I haven't the foggiest notion how old he is. Maybe a veterinarian could tell me. I'll have to look into it by and by. I've grown quite attached to him after all this time.

Rip is brave, and that's the truth. I've seen him flinch before he scrambles into a pile of burning rubble, but he goes in all the same. He puts up with smoldering debris, intense heat, thick smoke, and jets of water from the fire hoses and keeps going.

Once we tried to leave an area where the victims had already been removed. We figured our job was done, so Garrick and I picked up our shovels and started walking. But not Rip. He barked and began his little digging routine. He kept digging, and soon we could see the corner of what looked like a four-poster bed. We gave a shout for more help and quickly dug out a woman who had been sleeping in the bed. She was barely breathing by the time we got to her. If it hadn't been for Rip, that woman's fine four-poster would have been her deathbed and her casket, all in one.

An incident happened last week that gave us all a good laugh, and that's rare in these grim times. Rip was doing his little scrabbling and digging and uncovered a battered birdcage with a very vocal and frazzled parrot inside. The bird suddenly croaked, "Hey, mate, this is supposed to be my night out." I can tell you, we all hooted over that. Laughed so hard I almost cried.

Irwin carried the poor creature in his twisted cage to the nearest PDSA station so it could be cared for and, if necessary, a new home found for it. The incident lifted our spirits considerably. I guess we'll be sharing that story for the rest of the war.

Stay safe and well,

Brad

CHAPTER SIXTEEN

Tuesday morning Harriet woke up resolved to speak with Doreen about Bradley Welks and to ask Clarence Decker if he'd be willing to give Smoky a forever home. However, an emergency call regarding an acutely sick cria—a baby alpaca—changed her plans. Instead of visiting Doreen and Clarence, she spent much of the day tending to the small animal and working to save its life.

Bright and early Wednesday morning, Harriet got out of bed, still tired from the day before, but with the feeling of satisfaction that came from succeeding in a particularly difficult case for one of her patients. She attached Maxwell's prosthesis and opened the door so he could waddle outside while she got the coffee started. Charlie emerged soon after to complain about her empty food dish.

"All right, all right, give me a minute," Harriet told the cat, placing a hand over her mouth as she yawned. Yesterday had been stressful and physically demanding. Besides tending to the young alpaca, she'd dewormed an irritated donkey and set a bawling calf's broken leg. She'd missed lunch and had to make do with a protein bar.

Today she hoped to be able to drop by the Danbys' to tell Doreen about Bradley Welks's connection to someone named Malcolm Danby. She also wanted to show her the photocopies from the church records that Will had provided. Surely she was on the cusp of

MYSTERIES OF COBBLE HILL FARM

learning all there was to know about Rip and Bradley Welks and would soon be returning the collar and medal to their rightful owner.

A quick glance at the clinic calendar revealed two scheduled appointments for routine vaccinations first thing that morning, which should allow her to finish early and be on her way.

As she fumbled in the overhead cabinet for a clean mug, she recalled Monday night's conversation with Aunt Jinny and Polly regarding Mindy Milner, who'd bought all those pet supplies. Had she really bought the items for a friend? It did seem unusual, maybe even suspicious, as Polly had suggested. On the other hand, maybe there was nothing to it at all.

Thinking about it made her edgy. She'd also meant to call Van yesterday to ask about his progress in investigating Petey's abduction. When she did, should she mention the Milners?

Monday night, she'd been convinced that they should let the matter drop. Now she wasn't so sure, and she shouldn't ignore a viable lead, should she? Especially if she could save Van time by checking into it for him.

Harriet didn't like the idea of a local person being guilty of kidnapping Petey, but why would an outsider do so? The only possible motive she could think of involved keeping him from competing in the show at the end of the month. The note had hinted that Petey would be returned soon. But how soon was soon? Before the dog show? Not if she was right about why he'd been taken. The same thoughts kept playing over and over in her mind.

Please don't worry. Those words in the note suggested that the kidnapper had a conscience. Didn't it? It had been nearly a week since Petey's disappearance. The dog show in London was rapidly approaching. Was the timing of the dognapping coincidental, or purposeful? Either way, it was disturbing, and Harriet knew Gwen was quickly losing hope of ever seeing Petey again.

As Harriet poured herself a steaming cup of coffee, Maxwell scratched at the door to come in. She fed him and Charlie then went into the clinic to check on Smoky. The cat had made a quick recovery and would soon be ready for a new home.

She took Smoky out of the cage and gave him a quick cuddle. As she'd expected when she'd attempted an introduction between the two cats the other day, Charlie had taken an instant dislike to Smoky, hissing and arching her back in a manner most uncharacteristic of her usual disposition. So Smoky couldn't stay here. But would Clarence take the cat in?

After making her bed and dressing in jeans and a denim shirt with a white turtleneck underneath, Harriet poured herself a second cup of coffee and settled down to catch up on paperwork.

Polly breezed in with a bag of crullers from the bakery and gave her boss a suspicious look. "Glad I picked these up. You forgot all about breakfast, didn't you?"

Harriet chuckled. "Guilty as charged. What would I do without you?"

"Let's not find out. Come on, take one. The paperwork will still be there when you've eaten the most important meal of the day."

"I don't think this is quite the balanced breakfast most people have in mind when they say that." But Harriet obediently took a pastry, which was still warm, and bit into it.

"It's better than the nothing you've had," Polly retorted. She nodded toward Harriet's mug. "Or rather, just coffee." She helped herself to a cruller then asked, "Have you changed your mind about telling Van about the Milners?"

The bag of crullers attracted Maxwell's hopeful attention. He wagged his tail and gave them his best puppy-dog eyes, which both women ignored.

"I want to think about it some more," Harriet replied, pinching off another bite of cruller. "And I really want to tell Doreen about Bradley Welks's grave and his connection to Rip. I meant to do that yesterday, but I was so busy I could barely catch my breath."

"Did the baby alpaca make it?" Polly asked anxiously.

Harriet brushed the sugar from her fingers. "Yes. Maybe you could call out there later to make sure everything's going okay today. I'll take care of the appointments we have scheduled for this morning, and then I'll head over to the Danby place. If I have time, I'll call Van. I want to touch base with him anyway regarding his progress in locating Petey. I'll decide whether to mention the Milners to him between now and then."

It was after a hasty lunch—some yogurt and a handful of pistachios—that Harriet slid her phone into her purse and made sure she had the photocopies she wanted to show her friend.

"Hold down the fort, Polly," she called over her shoulder.

"Righto," Polly chirped.

As Harriet stepped outside, taking note of two unfamiliar vehicles parked next to her aunt's, her cell phone rang. Caller ID revealed it was Van.

"Hey, Van," she greeted him. "I intended to call you later today."

"Harriet, can you come to Gwen Higginbottom's house right now? You're not delivering a baby horse or something, are you?"

She didn't miss the seriousness underlying his humor. "It's convenient. Is this about Petey? Have you found him?"

"No, but Gwen has received something else in the post."

"Another note? A ransom demand at last?"

"It's a photograph," Van replied. "Please come as soon as you can. Gwen asked me to call you."

"Be there in one shake of a lamb's tail," she said, trying to keep her tone light and her attitude positive.

She thought she heard Van chuckle before the call was disconnected, and it eased the tight knot that seemed to clutch at her chest every time she thought of something horrible happening to Petey. She drove to Gwen's as quickly as the clunky old vehicle would allow, trying not to worry.

Van opened the door at her knock. He appeared serious but calm, and he ushered her into the sitting room.

Gwen sat on the sofa, clutching a large sheet of paper in one hand and plucking nervously at her tweed skirt with the other. Her eyes were wide with fright.

"Look," she whispered, offering the paper to Harriet.

Harriet gently took the sheet from her. She patted the woman's shoulder as she did so. It appeared to be a digital photograph printed on a sheet of regular printer paper. It was a close-up shot of Petey contentedly gnawing on a chew stick. Harriet could make out a bit of the plaid collar he always wore, but nothing about his surroundings. "Is this Petey?" she asked just to make sure.

"It is," Gwen replied.

"You're absolutely certain?" she pressed.

Gwen nodded. "That's his favorite kind of chew stick too, which is a lucky guess, unless someone went to the trouble of figuring it out by process of elimination. The photograph arrived in today's post. I called the detective constable right away."

Harriet examined the photo more closely. There were no words written on either side of the paper—simply a photo of Petey, apparently not in any distress.

"What does it mean?" Gwen asked.

Harriet and Van exchanged glances. "I think it means Petey is alive and well," Harriet declared.

Van nodded. "I think whoever has your dog is trying to reassure you that he's all right."

"No return address on the envelope again?" Harriet asked.

Van leaned over to pick it up from the end table. It was a large brown envelope with a clasp on the back. "No return address. Same postmark as before too," he added, passing it to Harriet for her perusal.

She immediately noticed that Gwen's name and address had been written in a more legible hand, not the childish scrawl like before. What did that mean?

"Do you think this is reassuring?" Gwen asked Harriet.

"I believe so." Harriet studied the photograph again. It was a bit grainy and dark, of course. Black Scotties didn't photograph well in most instances, and this wasn't exactly a high-resolution image. "Have you made any progress in tracking Petey down?" she asked Van.

Van shook his head. "I'm wearing out the leather on the bottom of my boots for nothing. You know, it's possible that Petey's not in the village or on one of the surrounding farms. Maybe someone from out of town took him. But who knows of him other than our locals?"

Harriet sat down next to Gwen on the sofa. "Out-of-towners who have competed against him and lost. I keep coming back to that as the one motive that makes sense—someone wants to make sure he's not in the London show. Gwen, do you know the names of the contestants entering a terrier in that show?"

"I know several of them personally," Gwen said, her expression lighter. "It would be easy enough to print off the list of those registered for the competition from the contest website. Do you really think someone snatched Petey so we couldn't compete?"

"I think that's a strong possibility, especially since the correspondence seems to indicate that whoever has him means to return him," Harriet replied. "I think maybe someone wants him out of the way so his own dog can win the top prize. But he loves dogs and doesn't want anything bad to happen to Petey."

Van snorted. "Aside from the theft of the dog being a criminal act, that's awfully poor sportsmanship."

Gwen's cheeks flushed with anger. "Indeed it is."

"Can you get the list for us?" Harriet asked.

Gwen sprang to her feet. "It won't take but a minute." She left the room with a slight spring in her step. Harriet wondered if she felt less helpless now that she had something to do.

Van stepped a little closer and said, "Doc, I have no jurisdiction outside our precinct, so I can't go running all over Yorkshire making inquiries. The most I can do is make some phone calls to other precincts to see if there have been any reported dognappings."

"I don't expect you to do any more than that. If Gwen calls a few people on the list to check on this, it'll give her something to do to keep her mind off missing Petey. And who knows? Someone might know something, though if someone she calls is guilty, I'd be shocked if they just came out and admitted it to her."

Gwen returned with the promised list.

Glancing quickly through the names and addresses, Harriet realized that terriers from all over Great Britain had been entered in the contest. Was it really feasible that someone as far away as Canterbury or Portsmouth had driven all the way to White Church Bay to steal Petey?

Handing the list back to Gwen, she said, "I think you should call the people you know first. Tell them what's happened to Petey. You might even warn them that their dogs could be taken before the competition too."

Gwen's eyes widened. "I hadn't thought of that. Do you think other people have had their pets stolen?"

"It's possible, isn't it? This seems like an isolated incident now, but if we broaden our search, we might find otherwise. And then we might find a pattern, which could help us catch whoever did this."

"I know most of the people on that list," Gwen said firmly. "The dog show world is a rather small one, really. We get to know one another rather well over the years. We won't let this dognapper get away with it."

"Excellent. I think you should make some phone calls," Harriet said. "But first, I want you to have a cup of strong tea with lots of sugar, and a good breakfast. Focus on eating some protein, like scrambled eggs. You're pale, and I suspect you're not eating well."

Gwen ducked her head. "I haven't been. I've been so worried about Petey that I haven't been all that hungry."

"Well, you'll need to keep up your strength if you're going to help us find him," Harriet said firmly, and Gwen squared her shoulders, a spark coming into her eyes. Harriet realized that the renewed hope and purpose in Gwen inspired her as well. No matter what, they would get Petey back.

CHAPTER SEVENTEEN

Immediately after leaving Gwen's, Harriet called Doreen to make sure she was at home.

"Come on over," Doreen said. "The kids are in school, and Tom's helping a neighbor fix his water pump. We'll have a nice cuppa and a cozy chat."

Harriet, her spirits lifted, stopped by the bakery for pastries to take with her. As she drove out to the Danby farm, nagging suspicions about Mindy Milner's recent purchase of pet supplies wriggled their way into her thoughts. Should she ask Van to pay the Milners a visit? She had no evidence at all that they'd done anything. Then again, they didn't have any real evidence against any of their other suspects. And truth be told, the Milners could have snatched Petey for someone else's benefit. That might be what Mindy had meant when she'd said she was buying "for a friend." But why on earth would they do such a thing? Would the job pay well enough to make it worth the risk?

With a sigh, Harriet decided she was too involved at this point and not thinking clearly. Still, she nursed a growing certainty that whoever had taken Petey was someone trying to eliminate the competition at the dog show, if only temporarily. She needed to discuss the matter with Van the next time she spoke with him.

Harriet knocked on the Danbys' door, and Doreen opened it and ushered her in, chatting merrily. "Let's sit in the kitchen," she suggested. "It's the perfect space on a chilly day like today."

Harriet followed her. The room was comfortable and smelled of something spicy and sweet.

"The kettle's on, and I made biscuits." Doreen indicated an array of ginger cookies cooling on the counter. Her gaze swiveled briefly to the white bakery box Harriet held in her hands.

"I brought something too," Harriet said, noting the glance.

"I'll never say no to anything from the Happy Cup," Doreen assured her. She lifted the lid and made a cooing sound. "I love banoffee pie."

Harriet smiled. "I thought so." She took a seat at the table and settled in for a comfortable chat. She noted the childish artwork on the front of Doreen's refrigerator and what appeared to be a math test featuring a perfect score.

"So how are the kids?" she asked.

"Growing like weeds," Doreen replied happily. "And eating me and Tom out of house and home. What's new with the search for Gwen's dog?"

"It's a long story," Harriet said. "And it seems to get longer, with no resolution in sight." She briefly explained how Gwen intended to call other participants registered for the upcoming competition to find out if their dogs had also been kidnapped.

"The task should keep Gwen occupied," Harriet added. "And who knows? Someone might provide a lead that would have Petey back home in no time. As I told Gwen, if someone really did take Petey to keep him from competing, other dogs may be in danger too. Van is going to call around to other precincts to see if any other show dogs have gone missing recently."

Doreen poured Harriet a cup of tea from a pot covered with a blue floral tea cozy. "Poor Van. Nothing like this has happened around here before. I doubt it's covered in the police manual."

Harriet nodded as she blew on her hot tea.

"If you think about it though, while kidnapping a dog to keep it from the show ring is unethical and criminal, it does make sense in a way," Doreen said. "I mean, it's a motive, right?"

Harriet agreed. "That's been my main theory."

"But what if it isn't that complicated?" Doreen continued. "I suppose someone could have simply fallen in love with Petey and wanted him for themselves. They then seized the opportunity when it was presented."

Harriet held up a finger. "You're forgetting the note promising Petey will be returned soon and that Gwen is not to worry."

"Yes, I did forget about that." With a frown, Doreen added, "I have a friend, Rachel, over in Bristol. She and her husband own two Cavalier King Charles spaniels. They're purebred, but not show dogs. Rachel and Chris never had children, so they've lavished all their love on their dogs."

Harriet nodded, though she was puzzled by how this tied in.

"One day, the dogs disappeared, and Rachel thought they must have run away even though they'd never done that before. No one could figure out how the dogs had gotten out of the fenced garden. She and Chris drove all around the neighborhood looking for them. They posted flyers, put an ad in the local paper, and even went door-to-door asking if anyone had seen them, but finally they had to give up and assume they were lost for good."

"How sad," Harriet murmured, trying to imagine how she'd feel if she lost Maxwell. And she'd only had him for a few short months.

"Two weeks later, they received a letter from a woman who said she'd discovered the runaways, taken them in, cared for them, fed them, the works. The woman explained she would be happy to return the dogs but she wanted to be reimbursed for her expenses."

"Naturally," Harriet said dryly.

"Rachel and Chris knew it was a scam. Their dogs had been abducted, but they knew there was no way to prove it. And they were so grateful to have them returned safely that they paid the woman. Do you think maybe that's what's happened to Petey? Not being held for ransom but some kind of extortion attempt?"

"No, that can't be it," Harriet mused. "In order for the scam to work, the woman who took your friend's dogs had to be able to say she didn't know whose dogs they were at first and that as soon as she found out who the owners were, she returned them. The person who took Petey can't claim he doesn't know who Petey belongs to. The letter and photograph Gwen received proves that."

Doreen sat up straight. "What photograph?"

"This morning Gwen received a photograph of Petey in the post. He appears to be happily gnawing on a treat."

"Proof of life?" Doreen asked, one eyebrow raised.

Harriet shrugged. "Proof of happiness, for all we know. Nothing was written on the back, no accompanying note. Just a digital photo printed on regular computer paper."

"Maybe the kidnapper thinks keeping in touch this way will keep Gwen from calling the police," Doreen suggested.

"Too late. The DC has already been investigating."

Doreen cut a piece of banoffee pie for Harriet and then for herself. "Enough about Petey. What about Rip? Dig up anything new there?"

Harriet grinned. "Funny you should ask." She rummaged through her purse, which she'd hung on the back of the chair, and retrieved the photocopies Will had given her. "Will found the information in some old church records kept by previous ministers. It appears that Rip and the man he belonged to might be somehow related to you—or Tom at least."

"What?" Doreen's eyes widened as she unfolded the papers and scanned them quickly. "This entry is dated 1945."

"Keep reading. Rip belonged to a man named Bradley Welks. He was living here in 1945. He died in 1963, as you'll see in one of the other entries. He was buried in the church cemetery. Someone named Malcolm Danby paid for the funeral services."

"I don't recall any Malcolms in the family."

Harriet took another sip of tea. "There must be a relation somewhere. Danby isn't that common a name."

"I'll ask Tom," Doreen said. "There are Danbys scattered all over the county, but the name Malcolm isn't ringing a bell." As she continued to peruse the pages, she smiled. "Says here that Bradley Welks and Rip opened the church fete that summer. Quite an honor in these parts and not bestowed lightly."

"That's what Pastor Will told me," Harriet said. "But considering Rip was presented with a Dickin Medal by the Lord Mayor of London, I'd say it was an honor well deserved."

"All right then, the collar and medal belonged to the dog, and the dog belonged to Bradley Welks." Doreen repeated this as though trying to get the information straight. "I'm afraid the name Welks doesn't ring a bell either. No Welkses living in the village now that I'm aware of."

"He might not have had a family of his own," Harriet pointed out. "Unless he was related to the man who paid for the funeral. Please check with Tom when you get a chance. I'd love to return the artifacts to someone in Bradley Welks's family."

"I'll do that, but this man Malcolm Danby is more than likely no longer alive," Doreen said.

"That's true, and I forgot to ask Will to see if Malcolm Danby is buried here too. If he is, he might have descendants living locally—an elderly child, perhaps, or grandchildren or even great-grandchildren."

Doreen smiled. "Odd how something that happened so long ago can still ignite a spark of interest today, isn't it? Now I'm eager to find out everything I can about this gallant Rip."

"Me too," Harriet said.

"I'm curious. Why are you so keen?" Doreen finished her pie and pushed the plate away. "This Welks chap is no relation to you, and this all happened long before you came to live here."

Harriet shrugged. "Must be my interest in history and my love of dogs. Ever since Van brought the collar and the medal to me, I've felt an obligation to see that they were returned to the rightful owner."

"All right then," Doreen said. "Tom and I will put our heads together and see what we can come up with." She dabbed her lips with a napkin. "It's a puzzle how those things ended up in the lost and found at the police station."

"I think that's odd too," Harriet said. "If someone discovered them in their attic or a closet, they would either keep them or throw them away. I still think they were buried at one time or another, because of the dirt packed into them."

"Yes, but even if they were buried and dug up, we still have the same question." Doreen frowned, clearly puzzled. "A person might show them to their friends and neighbors or other family members to see if anyone recognizes the names. Or just throw them away, like you said. But why take them to the police station? And then put them in the lost and found anonymously? Wouldn't they at least check with an officer to ask if that was the appropriate or helpful thing to do?"

"I agree. It's odd."

"And another thing," Doreen said. "I think we can rule out kids being behind it. If any of mine had found an old dog collar and a war medallion, they'd have kept them and shown them to their friends. Mine have what they call treasure boxes in which they keep all manner of bits and bobs. Even little Terrance has an old biscuit tin where he stashes pebbles, feathers, and other things that catch his eye. You'd think he had the crown jewels in there." She leaned back in her chair. "No, they would never have turned in such items to the police station. It's finders keepers with them."

"You're probably right," Harriet said.

"I know kids." Doreen paused, her teacup halfway to her lips. Then her eyes widened. "You think these items were buried at one time, right? Do you think they were buried with Mr. Welks?"

"I saw the grave, and it hasn't been disturbed," Harriet said. "Besides, it's more likely that they would have been buried with Rip, don't you think?"

Doreen considered this. "I suppose you're right. But why dig up a dog's grave?"

"I doubt it was done on purpose," Harriet said. "And after all this time, there was probably nothing in the dog's grave but those artifacts."

"Still a lot of unanswered questions, aren't there?" Doreen asked. "I mean, who found the items and where did he find them?"

Harriet drained the last of her tea and then declared, "I'm not giving up until I find out."

CHAPTER EIGHTEEN

The next couple of days passed in a blur. Besides tending to her animal patients, Harriet tackled neglected household chores, grocery shopping, and emails from people inquiring about purchasing prints of her grandfather's paintings. Mrs. Ida Winslow, who managed Harold Bailey's gallery, had gone away to visit family in Cornwall, so this task had fallen to Harriet, making her even more thankful that the busy tourist season was over.

On Saturday, Harriet managed to squeeze in a brief visit and a cup of tea with Gwen.

Calling the other dog owners registered for the upcoming London competition had not only given Gwen something to do to take her mind off her unfortunate predicament but had also garnered her sympathy from other dog owners, which helped her feel less alone and therefore bolstered her spirits.

"But, Harriet, no one else's dogs were taken," Gwen concluded.

"Have you spoken to everyone on the list?" Harriet asked.

"Not yet, but I have a feeling I won't find anyone else in the same situation as I am." She refilled Harriet's pink-and-yellow chintz teacup from a teapot covered with a bright pink tea cozy. Harriet thought of them as little sweaters. It seemed all the women in the village used them when the weather cooled so the tea would stay hot longer in the pot. "I may have to cancel my hotel reservation and notify the committee that I'm withdrawing Petey from the competition."

"Please don't do that yet," Harriet said. "There's still time. Maybe Petey will be returned before the dog show." She sincerely hoped so anyway. "Let me ask you something, Gwen. How likely is it that Petey would win the contest?"

After a pensive pause, Gwen replied, "I feel certain he'd win in his category, which means he'd move up to the final round. And there, he would have a very good chance of winning Best in Show."

"The people that you've spoken with on the phone," Harriet said. "If I asked them about Petey's chances of winning, what do you think they would say?"

Gwen smiled. "I don't think any one of them would say Petey is a *sure* winner. How could they? Each one wants his or her own dog to win, but they would probably all agree that Petey is the dog to beat. And the sort of folks who bet money on these things would put a small stake on Petey. I'm sure of it." Clearing her throat, she added, "He's won so many competitions before. Petey is what we call 'the favorite to win.'"

Harriet reached over to pat Gwen's hand. No doubt about it, the woman was a proud pet owner, and she deserved to be. "I believe you. Petey is the top contender. I think that's why he was taken in the first place, and I feel almost certain he'll be returned unharmed when the contest is over. However, we're not going to give up on trying to find him between now and then. Van is pursuing other avenues of investigation. You keep making your calls. After all, someone on that list could be the culprit, since those people have the most to gain by Petey missing the show."

"I don't want to believe that," Gwen protested. "It would be such poor sportsmanship. I've known most of these people for years. We're always meeting up at one competition or another. As I said before, the dog show world is not all that large. I can't wrap my head around any of them doing this to me."

Unfortunately, that didn't mean no one had, but Harriet didn't want to make the woman paranoid about her fellow competitors. By the time Harriet was ready to go, Gwen was determined to call the remaining names on the list. She reluctantly promised not to withdraw from the competition. At least not yet.

"Good. Don't cancel anything," Harriet said. "There's still a week left before the big show. Call me an optimist, but there's a chance we may recover Petey before then."

She still felt optimistic on Monday, which began with a dental checkup on a cute pug followed by numerous other routine visits for vaccines and heartworm medication. A vague notion about Petey's disappearance was slowly beginning to form in her brain. She couldn't quite put her finger on it, but she knew she would.

At three o'clock, Harriet asked Polly to fetch a cardboard pet carrier. "I'm taking Smoky to his new home. At least, that's what I hope I'm doing."

Polly chuckled. "Who's taking him in? Anyone I know?"

"With any luck, Clarence Decker. I haven't asked him yet, but when he sees the cat, I think he'll agree. I'm told he has a heart for strays."

Raising her eyebrow, Polly asked, "What will Rupert Decker say to that?" She held the box open while Harriet gently removed Smoky from his cage and placed him inside.

"I don't know what he'll say," Harriet said. "I've heard he's more like Clarence than we think. He likes animals better than people. Maybe he'll let his son take the cat in. It's worth a try."

"I suppose so," Polly said with a dubious frown as she closed the carrier. The cat gave an annoyed meow from within the container.

"Think of it this way," Harriet went on. "He's allowed Clarence to keep all those other animals in their garden. He pays for the supplies, the food, and all the rest of it. He's a carpenter, right? So he probably made those pens and hutches for his son too. Or maybe they made them together."

Polly considered this for a moment. "You're right. Perhaps his mean streak isn't as wide as we think."

Harriet hoped that was true. She slipped her purse over her shoulder and scooped up the carrier. Placing it on the floor behind the driver's seat of the Beast, she said a quick prayer that Clarence would already be home from school and that Rupert would not be there.

She rattled into town to make a quick stop at Pet Pangaea first. If she was going to saddle the Deckers with a new pet, the least she could do was supply them with some food and other essentials. She wasn't sure if Clarence already had a cat, and if not, he'd need a few items to care for Smoky properly.

Tamzin greeted her with a smile, wearing a pine-green corduroy skirt that fell to the top of her high leather boots. A wide belt with a gleaming buckle emphasized her waist. A matching green vest completed her outfit. Harriet once again marveled at the woman's flair for fashion.

She easily found what she was after, and as she piled her purchases onto the counter, Tamzin said, "Shopping for sweet Charlie, are you?"

It was one of the things that made Tamzin a successful businesswoman. She knew her customers as well as their pets and kept in stock the items people ordered over and over again.

"Not shopping for Charlie today," Harriet said. "These items are for a stray cat I treated. I'm hoping Clarence Decker will give the cat a permanent home."

Tamzin's expression registered both surprise and approval. "That's kind of you to provide everything he'll need." With a wink she added, "It might make it hard for the boy to say no when you're providing all the necessities. On the other hand, I've never known Clarence to turn away a creature that needed a home. He has a big heart, that one. I'll throw in a catnip toy on the house."

"How kind," Harriet said. "Thank you."

Tamzin smiled. "Clarence is one of my best customers, truth be told. Sometimes he even does odd jobs for me to earn a little cash to pay for what he needs. Over the years, he's had quite an assortment of animals. Don't know how he accumulates them all or how they find their way to him. Honestly, he's had everything from A to Z. Wouldn't be surprised if he now has an aardvark and a zebra." She laughed heartily, pleased with her own joke.

"I'm eager to see his animals," Harriet said. "When I was out there last week with Detective Constable Worthington, we didn't have an opportunity for a tour."

"What took you out to the Decker place?" Tamzin asked as she bagged Harriet's purchases.

"We were hoping to find Petey, Gwen Higginbottom's little Scottie. Remember? Jane Birtwhistle said she'd seen the dog abducted by a tall man in yellow rain gear. Rupert Decker's name was on my unofficial list of possible suspects."

"Yes, I remember," Tamzin said. "It was the day Gwen came in with the flyers. How's she doing?"

"The poor woman is beside herself, as you can imagine. Her whole world revolves around Petey. We're hoping to recover him before the big London dog show on Saturday."

Tamzin said nothing as she returned Harriet's credit card.

"It's too bad, really," Harriet went on. "Petey would probably win in his category and then advance to the final round. There's a good chance he could win Best in Show. He'd be the most famous dog in Great Britain for a year at least. And to think, he's a customer of yours."

With a weak smile, Tamzin said, "I didn't realize the competition was quite so soon. Gwen really has her heart set on winning, doesn't she?"

"Of course. And with only a few days left to help Petey recover from his adventure and go through his paces, Gwen's getting worried. If someone stole Petey to prevent him from competing, her hopes will be dashed. She's already considering canceling her hotel reservations."

"What a shame," Tamzin murmured. "Any idea who took the dog?"

"None. Some tall man with yellow wellies and matching rain gear. That's all Jane has been able to share with us."

Tamzin handed Harriet her bag. "Tell Gwen to keep her chin up. Petey may reappear sooner than later."

"I hope so. I really do." She wanted to ask Tamzin about Mindy Milner's recent purchases for a friend's dog, but would that be too nosy?

Before Harriet could make up her mind, the bell over the front door jangled, announcing the arrival of another customer. A woman entered, holding a small child by the hand. The toddler was so bundled up in a knitted hat and thick jacket that Harriet couldn't tell if it was a boy or a girl.

Tamzin thanked her then made her way around the counter to greet the newcomers and offer them help in finding what they needed. Harriet had the oddest feeling that Tamzin seemed anxious to avoid any further discussion about Gwen's dilemma. Or was she imagining things?

Harriet lifted the bag and left the store, stowing her purchases in the back seat. She could hear Smoky scrabbling around in the box, making irritable noises. He was one unhappy cat.

"We're almost there, Smoky. Hang on, buddy," Harriet said, attempting to soothe the fidgety feline. "I wanted to make sure you have everything you need for your new home."

On her way to the Deckers' house, she lifted up another silent, yet fervent, prayer that she'd be able to speak with Clarence alone and that the teenager would be ready, willing, and able to give Smoky a home.

CHAPTER NINETEEN

Harriet's mind wandered as she drove. She should have the furnace at home serviced before really cold weather set in. She also wondered if she should put in a supply of firewood. She was looking forward to cozy nights, curled up with a good book and a cup of hot tea while the flames danced in the fireplace. That meant she'd need to get the chimney checked out and make sure a bird or squirrel hadn't set up residence in there. Had Grandad used the fireplace much? She couldn't remember, since she'd mostly visited him in the summertime.

Smoky gave an annoyed yowl, snapping Harriet out of her reverie as she pulled into the Deckers' driveway.

As she'd hoped, Rupert's truck was nowhere in sight, but she caught a glimpse of Clarence at the side of the house carrying what looked like an armful of straw. He wore baggy jeans and a green flannel shirt with a gray T-shirt underneath. When Ivanhoe gave a bark announcing her arrival, Clarence glanced toward the drive then dropped the straw into a pen.

Harriet strained to get a glimpse of the animal inside. Was that a pygmy goat?

She exited the vehicle slowly in case the German shepherd went into watchdog mode. But Ivanhoe appeared to remember her and wagged his tail—not enthusiastically like Maxwell did, but friendly enough.

If Clarence was surprised to see her, he didn't show it as he approached.

Harriet called out a cheery hello then opened the back door of the Beast and removed the cardboard carrier with Smoky inside. She was delighted to catch the teenager alone and made up her mind to take care of business quickly so she could be on her way before Rupert returned.

Clarence raised a hand in greeting. When he caught sight of the carrier, interest brightened his face. Harriet tried not to smile. He had taken the bait. It was obvious he was eager to see what sort of animal she'd brought with her. As he drew nearer, she noted he wore hiking boots, not yellow wellies. She'd had a hard time imagining either of the Decker males in yellow outerwear anyway.

"What's in there?" He tipped his chin at the carrier.

There was something almost eager in his tone. When she caught a glimpse of concern in his blue eyes too, Harriet smiled. She felt they shared a love for God's creatures, making the two of them kindred spirits. She was suddenly determined to be friends with Clarence, no matter how rude his father might prove to be.

"I've got a homeless cat here," she told him. "A couple brought him to me when they found him doused in gasoline. Petrol, I mean. I've cleaned him up and checked him over. I've also given him the necessary vaccinations. I think he'll be fine now. But I need to find a safe place for him to live."

As the boy opened the box and removed the gray cat with a gentle but firm grip, she added, "I've been calling him Smoky. I think you can see why. Would you be willing to take him in?"

"He's a handsome one, he is," Clarence said, stroking the cat's soft fur. Smoky leaned into the attention, purring loudly.

"He is indeed." Harriet was pleased to see that the teen handled the cat with a calm and gentle expertise. "Do you think your father would allow you to keep him?"

Clarence's mouth quirked up on one side. "Dad doesn't care, as long as I keep the animals out of the house and care for them myself."

"But what about Ivanhoe? Isn't he a house pet?" Harriet gestured to the Alsatian.

With a chuckle, Clarence said, "Ivanhoe is Dad's dog. He's got the run of the place."

Harriet smiled. Then peering around the boy's tall, lanky figure, she asked, "So what do you have there in the yard? I've heard you have quite a menagerie."

His eyes lit up. "Come see." Still cradling Smoky in his arms, Clarence led the way around to the back of the house with long, quick strides.

Harriet, hurrying to keep up with him, was pleased to see how compliant Smoky was, apparently content to let Clarence hold him and stroke his smooth fur. She was glad to see that Smoky seemed to agree with her choice of home for him.

If she'd had any fears as to how well Clarence Decker cared for his strays, they evaporated as she took in the space. The pens, cages, and hutches that dotted the garden were well built and tidy. The water dishes were clean and the food trays as well. Each provided adequate shelter for the enclosed animal in case of bad weather.

The pen where he'd dropped the armful of straw contained a small pygmy goat with a leg expertly splinted.

"That's Geoffrey," Clarence said. "Broken leg. Belongs to a friend of mine. She couldn't care for him after he was injured, so I've taken him in until he's had time to heal."

From there, Clarence led Harriet from one cage to the next, introducing her to an assortment of sick or injured animals recovering in his care—a colorful male pheasant with a broken wing, a duck with a missing foot, and even an emaciated hedgehog.

"What happened to that little guy?" she asked. She hadn't seen many hedgehogs in Connecticut, but she'd come to admire the adorable creatures.

"Someone gave it to a kid as a pet." Clarence snorted. "The girl wasn't old enough to know how to care for him, and the parents were clueless. They didn't feed him or give him water. They treated him like a stuffed animal or something. I rescued him. I call him Henry the Eighth."

Harriet grinned. "You named your hedgehog after a king?"

Laughing, Clarence answered, "No, he's the eighth hoglet I've rescued."

Harriet was impressed. "I've been told you have a love of animals and that you're quite good with them. I see now that it's true. I was concerned that you might not really know how to provide adequately for the injured ones, but I was mistaken. You have a knack for this, Clarence. You'd make a good veterinarian if you chose to pursue that."

The boy blushed a deep red. He said nothing, but Harriet sensed he was pleased by the compliment.

"Where did you learn how to splint a goat's leg and rehydrate a hedgehog?" she asked, guessing that talking about his animals would make him more comfortable.

"From library books and videos posted online," Clarence replied. "Dad has offered suggestions from time to time."

"Really?" Harriet asked before she could stop herself.

"Sure," Clarence said, not sounding offended at all. "He's not so fond of people, as you've probably guessed, but he likes animals, and he's good with them. He just doesn't want them underfoot in the house."

"Good to know," Harriet replied. Glancing again at Smoky in the teenager's long arms, she realized she'd made a good choice in asking Clarence to take the cat.

Clarence saw her gaze and grinned. "You know, it wouldn't surprise me if Dad makes an exception for this fine chap."

"What makes you think that?"

"My mum kept a cat before she died. Dad didn't mind at all that it stayed inside with us. But Frisky died shortly after Mum, and we never got another cat—not a pet cat, anyway. We've had a few mousers and such, but I have a feeling Smoky and Dad will get along."

Harriet remained silent, taking in what he'd said. Maybe everyone was wrong about Rupert. Perhaps his sullen manner was really a kind of shyness around people. Maybe he still grieved the loss of his wife. Who knew? Whatever the reason, she was getting a whole new perspective on the Deckers, and she reminded herself to keep an open mind and form her own opinions about people in the future.

Clarence interrupted her thoughts. "When you came out the other day with that detective constable, you said you were trying to find a missing dog." He sounded concerned.

"We were. We still are. As we said, Gwen Higginbottom's Scottish terrier was abducted. He's been gone over a week now, and she's frantic."

Clarence met her eye squarely. "You came here because you thought Dad was guilty of something, didn't you?"

Harriet hesitated, not quite sure how to respond to that. She didn't want to lie to the boy, but she wasn't sure how truthful she should be.

But before she could answer, Clarence went on. "I knew it. As soon as I saw you and the copper, I knew you thought Dad had hurt Petey or taken him away somewhere."

"Your father's name came up as a possible suspect," Harriet finally admitted. "Because Miss Higginbottom complained about his work, some people thought your dad may have taken her dog for revenge. Also, an eyewitness saw a tall man take Petey from the garden. She couldn't identify him, but your father is tall. You're tall as well, so you made the list too."

Clarence's eyes widened. "Someone thought *I'd* steal a dog? One as famous as Petey?" He shook his head disbelievingly. "That's crazy. Dad would never hurt an animal. Neither would I. Especially little Petey. He's a champion, you know. We're hoping to watch him win the national competition on the telly."

Harriet felt a surge of happiness. "I'm glad to hear it. And you both had an alibi for the night in question, so we scratched your names off the list right away. It wasn't personal. And now that I've gotten to know you better, I can see you have the best intentions for animals."

"Glad of that," Clarence declared with feeling.

Mindful of the time, Harriet straightened. "I've got some supplies for Smoky in the back of my vehicle—food, a water bowl, and even a catnip toy that Tamzin at Pet Pangaea threw in free of charge when I told her I was bringing Smoky to you."

"Sure, I'll keep him. And gladly."

"Where will you put him until your father says he can stay in the house?" Harriet glanced around.

"See that?" Clarence tipped his head in the direction of a small shed. "There's an old doghouse in there. I can put a bed inside for the cat and keep his food and water and other things in there too until I find out which way the wind blows with my dad. Besides, it will give Smoky time to get used to me." He stroked the cat under its chin. Smoky purred, and Clarence chuckled. "We'll be fine, won't we, boy?"

Harriet smiled. "I think so too."

She drove back to the clinic, humming a praise tune in her happiness. No, she hadn't found Petey—yet—but she had shortened the suspect list and gained a young colleague at the same time. She lost herself in her thoughts, imagining the part she could play in encouraging Clarence to take school more seriously so he could become a veterinarian. She could mentor him as he worked at the clinic after school and on weekends, and when he graduated from veterinary school, he would announce in his valedictory speech that he owed it all to Harriet Bailey...

Okay, maybe that was a bit much. But a girl could dream, couldn't she?

London

August 1944

Dear Malcolm,

Paris is liberated at last! I'm not telling you anything you don't already know, I'm sure. Every paper in the kingdom printed the news on the first page. You should have heard the church bells ringing all together. A glorious sound! Not sure if I mentioned before that it was agreed upon early in the war that all church bells in London would be silenced. No ringing for weddings or other services—only in case of in invasion, and then all bells would ring to sound the alarm. That ban was lifted for certain occasions in 1942, and thankfully the invasion never came.

Garrick and I are hoping that between our forces and the Americans, we'll soon bring Hitler to his knees.

Those of us in the ARP are still busy, but not so frantic like before, during the blitz. If they can spare me, I might be able to come help you with the barley harvest. If I come, I'll be bringing Rip along. I want you to meet my fine four-legged buddy.

And speaking of Rip, guess what? He's been nominated for a medal. That's something, that is! If the War Office approves the nomination, Rip will receive what they call the Dickin Medal. Guess they started handing them out last year to animal heroes going above and beyond the call of duty. Rip is surely deserving. He's already a hero in my book, and every man Jack at the station thinks so too. We've seen the little guy in action. Hard to believe, but Rip has been directly responsible for rescuing more than a hundred souls so far. How many more might he rescue between now and the time this war comes to an end?

Remember I mentioned the PDSA, that charity for sick and injured animals? They're the ones sponsoring the award. They've even been fundraising with some of the other dogs that have played their part in the war. People want to meet the dogs, to hear how they've been serving king and country. Some of the dogs even get their pictures in the papers with nice write-ups about their bravery and devotion to duty.

Well, there's none more dutiful than Rip, and I'm not shy about saying so. All of us at the station are delighted that he's been nominated. I don't know for sure if or when he'll get the medal. If I'm in White Church Bay when the call comes through, we'll need you to take us to the station, and we'll catch the train back to London so Rip can have his day in the spotlight.

I've read that this Dickin Medal has been awarded already to three messenger pigeons. Birds! What do you think of that? One of them, by the name of Tyke, was honored for flying over one hundred miles and delivering a message under difficult circumstances that led to the rescue of an RAF air crew. Another one was Winkie. He flew 120 miles to take a message from a crew in a downed bomber to his owner, who alerted the airbase. They knew from the note attached to Winkie's leg what time the plane went down, and after taking into account the wind speed and how long it took for Winkie to reach home, they were able to locate the plane and get help on its way within fifteen minutes of the bird's arrival. That's something, that is. Almost hard to believe. Not sure how they calculate such things, but I'm taking their word for it.

Of course, it's all well and good to honor these war birds, but there's no recipient who deserves the honor more than Rip, and I'll say so to any man's face. I don't think the average person has any idea how hard Rip and the other rescue dogs have worked. Honestly, I think they all deserve medals.

I went over to the Singing Canary again to see Cecily and enjoy some beans on toast. Had a fresh tomato with it too. While I was there I met Cecily and Irwin's young niece. Sweet lass, about fifteen years old. Name of Daphne. She works as a machinist repairing bullet holes in military uniforms so the clothes can go back to the troops.

Daphne told us how harrowing it is when the sirens start and they all traipse into the basement. They sit down against the wall, trembling with fear. Then as soon as the raid stops, she and the other girls return to their machines as though nothing happened. She says she'll never be able to hear a siren again, even that of a fire engine or ambulance, without a cold knot of fear forming in the pit of her stomach.

Thinking back, I wonder how Daphne or any of us ever got through the worst of it. Especially the youngsters and the old folks. The blitz was traumatic. How could it not be, seeing people you've known all your life killed, burned, maimed, and buried in the rubble of nearby houses?

Don't reckon I'll soon forget any of it either, watching the V-1s, the so-called doodlebugs, rattle across the skies every day. I always held my breath in terror. Either they'd drop straightaway and then I'd have my work cut out for me, or they'd sail silently on. That meant they'd fall on someone else, of course, but I'd find myself breathing again.

Some of the bombs have been duds. There's a disposal squad still going about making the bombs safe. We had to evacuate several families over on Bazeley Street until the squad could come and take care of one that landed—unexploded—in a garden. The families dutifully took their pallets and slept on the platform of Southgate Tube station. Wonder what passengers thought when they stepped off the trains and were forced to step around sleeping families sheltering there?

I'll keep you posted about the possibility of my getting leave. I'll try to find out more about Rip's award—if he's going to get it and when. Maybe you and the missus and the kiddies could travel to London with us for the ceremony? That would be something to remember, that would.

Your cousin,

Brad

CHAPTER TWENTY

On Tuesday morning, Doreen barreled through the front door of the clinic. Her face was flushed, and her wide eyes sparkled. The knitted scarf around her neck hung at odd angles. Her heavy pullover sweater appeared to be inside out. "Harriet, you won't believe this! We've found some old letters in the attic. You've got to read them. They tell the whole story of Rip and Bradley Welks and Tom's Uncle Mick and the Dickin Medal—*everything*."

She came to a halt and flushed even deeper as she apparently noticed the thin woman beside Polly's desk with a quivering Maltese in her arms. "Oh, I beg your pardon. I was so excited that it didn't even occur to me this might be a bad time for you."

Harriet came to her rescue. "It's all right, Doreen. They've finished their appointment and are on their way out." Harriet opened the door for the woman holding the dog, thanked her for coming, and reminded her to return for the follow-up appointment they'd scheduled.

The woman sidled out the door, casting an amused glance at Doreen on her way out.

With a flutter of excitement, Harriet turned to Doreen. "Let's talk about this over a hot drink. You can come too, Polly, if you want."

"Let me take care of this payment first," Polly said. "I'll meet you in there."

Harriet led Doreen into the kitchen. "Coffee's hot, or would you rather have tea?"

"Coffee will be fine," Doreen assured her. "I'm dying to show you these letters."

"And I'm dying to read them," Harriet said. At long last, some explanation for the collar and medal was coming to light. She inhaled the invigorating aroma of the coffee as she poured it into mugs for herself and Doreen. She joined Doreen at the table and set a mug in front of her. "Okay, let's see those letters. Take me through it from the beginning."

"After we spoke last time, I had a long talk with Tom. I told him everything you'd told me about Bradley Welks and the collar and the medal. I showed him the photocopies from the church records that Will shared with you. Tom had a vague recollection of a great-uncle named Malcolm Danby, so he made a few calls to some other relatives and pieced together that Malcolm Danby and Bradley Welks were cousins."

"That's one mystery solved," Harriet said. "I wondered why Malcolm paid for Bradley's funeral. It makes sense if they were family."

Doreen offered Harriet a small packet of envelopes held together with a rubber band. "There are six letters. Tom found them crammed in one of those narrow slots in an old rolltop desk in our attic, along with old recipes and sales receipts and such. Much of it dated back to World War II. His grandparents lived in our house before they retired and moved to Brighton."

"I'd hoped there was some connection between your husband and Bradley Welks," Harriet said. As she carefully tugged one of the old letters from its wrinkled envelope, her heart gave a twist. She couldn't believe she was holding history in her hands.

"They tell a story, those letters. Bradley Welks lived in Poplar at the time. It's a district in East London," Doreen explained.

Polly bustled in and caught the tail end of the conversation. "What did I miss? I heard you say these old letters were written by Bradley Welks. And they're all about Rip?" She helped herself to coffee and sat next to Harriet.

"That's right. They're written to a great-uncle of Tom's named Malcolm, who was Bradley's cousin. Tom and his relatives compared notes and pieced together some facts about Bradley. He never married. They thought he might have been handicapped in some way because he didn't join the war effort as a soldier, but the letters explained how Bradley served even though he was missing fingers. After Bradley died, Malcolm and his family moved to Canada sometime in the early seventies. Malcolm sold his farm—a small holding containing some sheep and an apple orchard—to another distant Danby cousin. Before he moved, he auctioned off a lot of furniture and other things that didn't make sense to drag across the ocean. We believe Tom's grandparents purchased his desk, and that's how the letters ended up in our attic."

Harriet began skimming the letters. "Rip was a stray. It's amazing how he went from that to a decorated war hero."

Doreen leaned forward. "Keep reading. Rip rescued a hundred people buried in the rubble in just one year during the blitz. He wasn't even a trained search and rescue dog. Just a lonely, hungry little stray."

"It's truly miraculous what animals can do," Harriet mused.

"Tom found a newspaper photo of Rip among the letters and showed it to the kids. They're enchanted with the story. Ella wants to take the collar and medal to school for show and tell. You didn't want them back right away, did you?"

"No," Harriet assured her. "My intent was to return them to someone related to Bradley Welks, and here you are. It seems appropriate, since you have the letters explaining what they're all about." She gave her friend's arm a squeeze. "I couldn't have asked for a happier ending. I can't wait to tell Van and Will."

She settled down to read the rest of the letters, passing them to Polly when she finished each one. Harriet found herself completely wrapped up in the past. She felt as if she'd known Bradley Welks personally, and she completely fell in love with Rip, the heroic little dog who had come so far.

After a while, Doreen said, "Tom is wondering if we should donate the items along with the letters to the Imperial War Museum or the historical society in York. What do you think?"

"I don't know. I think you should keep them," Polly said. "You can pass them down to your children and grandchildren. That way your family will always know Rip's story."

Harriet wasn't sure if either museum would truly appreciate the donation. The items probably had more sentimental than historical value. But she didn't want to influence Doreen one way or the other in such an important decision. "Do what feels right to you. But I will say you don't have to make that decision anytime soon. You can take some time and think about it."

"That's true," Doreen said. "We can discuss it as a family next time we're all together." She sighed. "Think of all the people alive today in London and elsewhere who have Rip to thank for rescuing their grandmas or great-uncles or parents. It wasn't just those hundred people and all the others he saved. It was everyone who came after them."

"It really is amazing when you put it like that. Not all heroes are human. Some of the best have four paws or wings." Harriet gave a silent prayer of thanksgiving for the little stray that had followed Bradley Welks to the air warden station that fateful day.

"That's right," Polly agreed. "Good old Rip."

"Harriet, you have no idea what you've started," Doreen told her. "Tom's been on the phone to faraway cousins he hasn't talked to in years and years. Suddenly, they're all interested in the family genealogy and trying to get in touch with kinfolk they've lost track of. Mostly the older uncles and aunts. Everyone wants to hear their stories now."

"That's wonderful," Harriet said. "Maybe there are other stories you're not aware of, perhaps some as exciting as Rip's story."

"Who knows? But we're going to find out. Harriet, you solved a mystery and brought a family closer together." Doreen beamed at her.

"I think that second part is the more important," Harriet said.

Polly chuckled. "So Rip's a Danby then. Treating him like a member of the family, are you?"

Doreen nodded. "An important member of the family too, I might point out. The kids are thrilled to have a famous dog in the family. Not everyone can boast that they have a pet awarded a medal for gallantry."

"It's brilliant," Polly said with a smile. After taking a sip of coffee, she added, "At least that's one mystery cleared up. Now we know all about the collar and the medal."

"Not quite," Harriet objected. She leaned an arm against the table and frowned. "We still don't know who put them into the lost and found. And we don't know where they were found or when or how."

"Tom insists we pursue the answers to those questions," Doreen told her. "He wants to pick up where your investigation has gotten us so far."

"I'm glad," Harriet said. "I hate loose ends."

"Of course, we have no idea how to go about finding those answers," Doreen added. "Any suggestions?"

Polly shrugged, and Harriet said, "Not a clue."

Doreen rose from the table. "Well, I'm not going to let it go. I need to thank whoever helped reunite our family, and I won't rest until I do."

CHAPTER TWENTY-ONE

The following morning, Harriet began her day early with a brisk walk along the bluffs, accompanied by Aunt Jinny. The weather was perfect, neither too hot nor too cold. The breeze teased a few strands from her ponytail. Harriet brushed them away, saying, "I have another idea about Petey's disappearance. I tossed and turned all night long thinking about the possibility, and it seems to me like a good lead to follow."

"What's that?" Aunt Jinny asked.

"It's only a suspicion," Harriet hurried to say. "I have no proof whatsoever, just a little nagging tug in that direction."

Aunt Jinny clasped Harriet's elbow. "Don't keep me in suspense. Tell me."

"Tamzin Pickers."

Her aunt's eyes widened with surprise.

Harriet remained silent, letting her process the idea.

Finally, Aunt Jinny asked, "How did you come up with that conclusion?"

"It isn't really a conclusion," Harriet insisted. "It's a suspicion, nothing more. Remember that photo of Petey gnawing on the chew stick? That's what gave me the idea that it might be Tamzin."

"I don't see the connection," Aunt Jinny said, a puzzled look on her face.

Harriet tried to explain. "Gwen mentioned that the chew stick was Petey's favorite kind. Who would know better than the shopkeeper who sells Petey's favorites what he likes best?" She cast her aunt a sidelong glance. "I admit, it's a rather feeble connection, but it's there."

"It makes sense in a way," her aunt agreed.

Encouraged, Harriet hurried on, eager to explain further. "Tamzin is also quite tall. She's the sort of fashion-minded person who would have yellow rain gear with matching boots and a slouch hat. Her shop is right down the street from Gwen's place, and she's comfortable around animals. She's probably met Petey, so he'd be used to her. And Jane didn't see a face, so maybe she just assumed it was a man carrying Petey away and she was mistaken."

"Do you have any idea where Tamzin was when Petey was taken?"

"No," Harriet admitted. "But I think someone should ask her."

Aunt Jinny heaved a sigh as she slowed her steps to a more leisurely pace. "But why would Tamzin kidnap Petey? What possible motive could she have?"

"I don't know that either. When I was in there the other day buying stuff for Smoky, I mentioned how much Gwen was grieving her pet and that she was thinking of withdrawing from the London competition. It seemed to affect Tamzin. Her reaction just seemed off to me. I can't quite put my finger on how though."

"Anyone with an ounce of empathy in their veins would feel sorry for Gwen in her present predicament," Aunt Jinny pointed out.

"True, but it sure looked like more than that." Harriet thrust her fists into the deep pockets of her jacket. "Maybe I imagined her reaction. I don't know. I'm probably grasping at straws."

"If Tamzin took the dog, then she must have also sent the note and the photograph," Aunt Jinny mused.

"I thought of that too."

"That means she intends to return the dog soon," her aunt went on. "But why she'd disguise her handwriting to look like a child's is beyond me."

"I think we just have to assume whoever did that was trying to really throw us off the scent." Harriet refused to give up on her new hypothesis so soon.

"But we keep coming back to motive. Does Tamzin have one?"

"That's why I hope to speak with her again—if we can't figure out the motive, we can at least see if she had opportunity. I'd like to try to uncover where she was that Thursday night," Harriet said. "I want you to come with me, if you're willing."

"Me?" Aunt Jinny stopped in midstride.

"I need a witness," Harriet said.

"Why not take Van?"

Harriet shook her head adamantly. "Say I bring a detective constable along. That would make it an official visit. If Tamzin admits in front of Van that she took Petey, he might be obligated as a police officer to press charges or something. She's probably much less likely to confess to him and risk that than she is to confide in a couple of friends."

"I see your point." They walked on in silence, making their way back home. Then Aunt Jinny asked, "You really don't expect to find

Petey at Tamzin's house, do you? They live on a crowded street crammed cheek to jowl with their neighbors. Someone would have heard the dog barking or would have seen him outside. Tamzin has no garden. She'd have to take Petey on a walk every day, probably multiple times a day. With all the flyers scattered around town and people keeping an eye out for Petey, the secret would have come out by now."

"That's a good point," Harriet said. "If she took Petey, she must have stashed him somewhere else, though I have no idea where. Like I said, this is merely a hunch. But the only way to know whether it's right or not is to follow up on it."

"Okay, I'll go with you," Aunt Jinny said.

Harriet caught the hint of reluctance in her tone. "It's important. For Gwen's sake. She'll be devastated if she doesn't get Petey back in time for the London dog show. They've both worked hard for this opportunity."

"I understand. Are we going to corner Tamzin at her shop, or at home?"

"We aren't going to corner her," Harriet protested. "This will be a neighborly visit at her house. I don't intend to accuse her of anything. I'm simply going to urge her to tell us if she knows anything at all about Petey's disappearance."

"It's going to be awkward," Aunt Jinny predicted. "Maybe we should ask Will for his advice on the matter."

Harriet considered it. Will was a good-natured man full of godly wisdom. He might indeed have a suggestion or two for the best way to approach the conversation with Tamzin. "I agree. We'll give him a call."

"I'd prefer to speak to him in person about this," Aunt Jinny told her.

Harriet shrugged. "If you insist."

"I do. This is a tough situation, make no mistake about it."

Later that afternoon, after both Aunt Jinny and Harriet had taken care of their respective patients, they made their way to the rectory. Will had responded to a text from Harriet that he would be free to speak with them any time after four o'clock. Harriet had thanked him, explaining that it was a matter of some urgency.

Aunt Jinny frowned when Harriet told her this. "Is it truly urgent? I hope Will isn't alarmed."

"It is urgent," Harriet insisted. "The hours and the days are ticking by. As a physician, you must surely be concerned about how the stress and anxiety may be affecting Gwen's health."

Aunt Jinny nodded. "I see your point."

Will met them at the front door of the rectory with a chocolate bar in his hand. Seeing them eyeing his afternoon snack, he quipped, "'Man does not live by bread alone.'"

Harriet laughed.

He ushered them into his private office. "Please make yourselves comfortable. Now, what is this urgent matter you want to speak about?"

"I'm hoping to get your guidance about a hunch I've developed regarding Gwen Higginbottom's missing Scottish terrier, Petey,"

Harriet said. She gave Will the reasoning she'd shared with her aunt that morning.

As she spoke, Will watched her attentively. He didn't interrupt, nor did he appear skeptical. She realized that simply laying it out for him made her feel better, as so often happened when confiding in a trusted friend. By the time she concluded, "I think Tamzin Pickers may have been the person who took Petey," the tension had seeped from her shoulders and the anxiety had left her voice.

"So you came to this conclusion based mainly on the chew in the photo Gwen received?" Will clarified.

"Mainly," Harriet affirmed. "But Tamzin's manner the other day also struck me as odd. She seemed strangely antsy about the subject and acted like she didn't want to talk about it. She could have been preoccupied with something else, of course, but still."

After a moment of consideration, Will said, "A strong hunch is worth following up. But what possible motive could she have for taking the dog?"

Harriet grimaced. "I can't think of a good reason. That's why I need to talk to Tamzin. I need to follow through on my suspicions."

"I agree," Will said slowly. "I agree that's the best way to move forward. How can I help?"

"I was hoping you could give me some advice on how to go about the conversation itself. Should I confront her right away with what I know? Or play dumb and see if she confesses?"

Will pondered her request for a moment. "Honesty is the best policy, and I don't think you need to accuse her forcefully. Sit down with her as we're doing now and explain everything the way you did with me. Tell her you can't let go of the feeling that she knows something about the abduction. No need to accuse her of having taken the dog. See how she responds to that. Your tone will be everything. You'll want to make sure she knows you're there as her friend and that you're simply trying to reunite a woman with her dog, not malign her character or anything. Coming from a place of kindness will be crucial."

"I think we should point out our concerns for Gwen's health as well," Aunt Jinny put in. "This has been extremely stressful for her. She's a patient of mine, and I've noticed the strain this has put on her. If it continues, it could have lasting effects."

"Point that out as well," Will agreed. "Tamzin is not heartless. If she indeed took Petey for some reason, your perspective and concern for a friend may make her come to her senses and return the dog." Then with a half-smile, he added, "At least we can pray that happens."

"Do you think I should explain that we came without the detective constable because we don't intend to encourage Gwen to press charges, that we simply want the dog back?" Harriet asked.

"You could do that. Also, press upon Tamzin that Gwen has her heart set on being in the competition," Will added. "When I visited with Gwen last week, she told me how important this competition is to her. She and Petey have prepared a long time for this. It would be a shame if she is forced to withdraw."

"Thank you, Will. You've been a big help," Aunt Jinny said, smiling at him.

"Yes, thank you," Harriet added. "I've been praying about what to say to Tamzin and how to say it. I wasn't sure if I wanted to be confrontational or not, but what you've said has helped me see that it's better to try to get her to open up to me."

"Speak your concerns in love," Will said. "If Tamzin is indeed the culprit who took the dog, I doubt she did so with malicious intent. She's not that sort of person."

His words rang true to Harriet. She hadn't exactly thought of that, but reflecting on what she knew of the pet store owner, Tamzin was not a bad person. She loved animals. She was generous when it came to supporting school fundraisers, church activities, and local charities. Every time Harriet went into the pet shop, she'd see a flyer advertising another fundraising event.

"Do you want me to come with you?" Will asked.

"Thank you for the offer. Normally I would take you up on it, but in this case I worry that Tamzin would be intimidated if we show up on her doorstep with you. She might feel more ganged up on with three of us. This is a casual, private conversation with two friends. If you're there, she might think we expect a full confession or something, but I simply want to hear what she has to say for herself. For all I know, she's totally innocent and has an alibi for the night in question." Harriet stood and gathered her jacket and bag.

"I suggest you approach her as soon as possible," Will went on. "The longer you avoid talking to her, the more difficult it will be when you do. Besides, as Jinny says, this has been hard on Gwen's nerves, and there's a deadline in the form of the dog show."

"My stomach is tied up in knots over it," Harriet admitted.

"I can understand that," Will said, giving her a sympathetic smile. "Perhaps if you start out by telling Tamzin you're concerned for Gwen, it might be easier to go on from there. You'll capture her empathy right away, I should think."

"Or prick her conscience," Aunt Jinny added as she too rose to her feet.

"Speaking of consciences, why do I feel guilty about this?" Harriet asked. "I've done nothing wrong. I'm just trying to help a friend. I'm following a hunch, is all."

"No one wants to risk making someone they like feel bad," Will told her. "Besides, most people don't like confrontation of any sort. Sometimes, however, we must care enough to confront."

"All right then," Harriet said, looking first at Will and then her aunt. "Let's go this evening after dinner, before I lose my nerve. We'll speak to her privately at her home. No need to bring her husband into this. He might not know what's going on."

Will rose and took each of them by a hand. "Let's pray that all goes well."

CHAPTER TWENTY-TWO

After a quick supper of scrambled eggs with mushrooms and toast, Harriet met her aunt in the parking area outside their homes. Harriet had been so nervous and edgy she could barely eat, and the food had tasted like sawdust.

Aunt Jinny seemed to sense her mood and offered to drive. Harriet willingly agreed, reluctant to drive in her distracted condition.

"Take a deep breath, my dear. It's going to be all right."

Harriet responded with a feeble smile. She sincerely hoped it *would* be all right. She had conjured so many possible scenarios of how Tamzin might react when they showed up on her doorstep unannounced to discuss Petey's disappearance. She didn't want to hurt the woman's feelings or cause a rift in their relationship.

"Do you think we should have called first?" Harriet asked.

"I thought so initially. But I was afraid she might put us off or make some sort of excuse why we shouldn't stop by this evening. Are you having second thoughts?" Aunt Jinny asked.

"No. Even if Tamzin didn't take the dog, I have a feeling she knows who did. It's that chew being Petey's favorite." She stared into the dark, inky night in which neither stars nor moon were visible. Harriet felt certain that Petey's whereabouts would be revealed tonight, though she couldn't say how she knew.

Recollecting Will's quiet prayer, she felt a sudden calmness. The knot in her stomach began to release. Everything would be all right.

The ride was a short one, and they soon reached the street where Tamzin lived, which glowed with golden light from the houses and those shops still open for business. Aunt Jinny found a parking space not too far from Tamzin's home then met Harriet on the sidewalk. Sliding her arm through Harriet's, she said, "All right then, let's do this. For Gwen's sake."

"And Petey's. He probably misses Gwen as much as she misses him." Harriet rapped the simple brass knocker against the door twice.

Aunt Jinny leaned in close to whisper, "Remember, 'speak the truth in love.'"

Before Harriet could respond, the door was opened by Tamzin herself. As usual, the tall woman was fashionably dressed in leggings and a floral tunic. She held a dish towel in one hand. The glimpse of domesticity caught Harriet off guard at first, but then she quickly reminded herself that even fashionable businesswomen had to wash their dishes.

Tamzin's expression of mild astonishment shifted quickly to one of caution as she greeted her unexpected guests. "Doctors, to what do I owe the pleasure?" She gave them a tight smile.

Harriet mustered a polite smile of her own. "Good evening, Tamzin. We'd like to speak with you about a private matter."

"And we'd prefer not to do it out here on the doorstep," Aunt Jinny added. She glanced around the street, as if watching for neighbors who might have spotted their arrival.

"Come through then," Tamzin said, somewhat reluctantly. "Follow me."

She led the way to a small sitting room with hardwood floors, brown leather club chairs, and custom ottomans. Ivory wallpaper with a pattern of trailing ivy lined one wall. The fireplace had been converted to gas. Several framed photos graced the mantel—Tamzin's children and grandchildren, Harriet supposed. There was a large glass case filled with tiny porcelain dogs and cats, giraffes, birds, and other animals. Apparently, Tamzin was a collector. In the distance, Harriet could hear a television and concluded that this tasteful room was for guests. Roger Pickers was probably lounging in another room, watching the telly and digesting his supper.

Tamzin indicated two of the chairs and then took a third. When all three were seated, she dropped the dish towel on the small round coffee table and clasped her hands in her lap. "Now what's all this about?"

Harriet glanced at her aunt, who gave her a reassuring smile and a nod. Swallowing the lump in her throat, Harriet began, "It's about Gwen Higginbottom."

This appeared to catch Tamzin off guard. She frowned. "Is she okay? What's happened?"

"She hasn't been herself since her dog, Petey, went missing," Harriet replied.

"We're concerned about her physical health and her mental well-being," Aunt Jinny added. "The stress and anxiety are taking a toll."

After a heavy pause, Tamzin cleared her throat. "So why have you come to me? I'm not a doctor or a counselor."

Harriet heaved a sigh. *Here goes.* "We believe you can tell us where Petey is."

There was a longer pause this time before Tamzin asked coldly, "And why do you think I would know?"

"Because of the chew in the photo with Petey. Other than Gwen, you're probably the only person who would know Petey's favorite treat."

Tamzin's face blanched. She clasped her hands so tightly they changed colors too. "How long have you known?"

"Not long," Harriet said gently. "We don't want to notify the police, but it's past time to return the dog to Gwen. This has gone on long enough."

Tamzin nodded sheepishly and ran a hand through her well-coiffed hair. It stood up like a bird's nest on one side. "I have a good excuse. Truly I do."

"I'd like to hear it," Aunt Jinny said crisply.

Tamzin shrank in her seat. "I knew I'd gone too far when you came in that day to buy the things for the stray cat, the one you were taking to the Decker boy. Is Gwen very angry with me?"

"She has no idea that we've come to see you, and I seriously doubt she even suspects you of stealing her dog. Ever since Jane said she saw a tall man that night, Gwen has fixated on that," Harriet told her.

Aunt Jinny leaned forward. "Why did you do it?"

"And where is Petey?" Harriet added.

"He's at my daughter's house over in Whitby. Safe and sound, I can assure you," Tamzin hastened to add. "Let me explain. My ten-year-old granddaughter Phillipa—Pip for short—was seriously injured a few weeks ago by a hit-and-run driver. She suffered a concussion, a broken ankle and femur, and then developed an abscess in her spinal cord. We're all grateful she's alive, but Pip's spirits are suffering. The poor thing has been in a wheelchair and unable to attend school. She's been bored and missing her friends."

"I hope she's making a sound recovery," Aunt Jinny said.

"The doctors say she'll probably be paralyzed for life," Tamzin said softly. "She's depressed, as you can imagine. The one thing that brings her joy is her Scottish terrier, Lady. Pip has suddenly become obsessed with wanting Lady to have puppies. She's been reading about dog breeding online, and her father checked out some books on the subject from the library for her."

Harriet shifted her gaze to a porcelain border collie in the glass case. She knew where this discussion was going and could almost sympathize with Tamzin's efforts to bring some joy into her granddaughter's life, especially when much of it had been taken away so cruelly.

"But what has this to do with Petey?" Aunt Jinny prompted.

"I thought if I could borrow Petey for a week or two, he might mate with Lady. There would eventually be puppies to keep her mind occupied and bring her a little happiness in the midst of her troubles." Tamzin's shoulders slumped. "A few months ago, I asked Gwen about the possibility of Petey mating with Lady, and the stud fee she quoted was so high, there was no way we could do it. So I decided to borrow him temporarily. I know now I went about it all wrong. It was daft. I feel like an idiot."

Harriet shook her head. "You could have explained all this to Gwen. She's a reasonable woman. You could have come to some financial agreement, I'm sure."

"I know, I know." Tamzin massaged her temples. "I must have been barmy. I don't know what I was thinking. I saw Petey that night with his nose pressed against the gate, his eyes twinkling with merriment, and I didn't even think twice. I simply took him. If you could have seen the color come back into Pip's cheeks when I brought him to the house, you'd understand. If you could see the happiness in her eyes when she talks about Lady having puppies..."

"But you must have known the London dog show is coming up," Aunt Jinny reminded her. "Gwen is considering withdrawing from the competition, and it would be a real shame if she did."

"Like I told Harriet the other day in the shop, I didn't realize it was coming up so soon," Tamzin said.

"I suppose you thought sending the note would ease her anxiety," Harriet said. "Is that why you sent it?"

Tamzin shook her head. "I didn't write it. Pip did. I didn't know she had until after it was mailed. I meant for her to send a thank-you note after I returned Petey, but she got ahead of me. She told me that if someone had Lady, she would like a letter telling her that Lady was doing well and would be home soon. I couldn't argue with that, and she begged me to send a picture of Petey too, so I sent the photo. I wanted Gwen to know that Petey was alive and well, not being caged in some dreadful puppy mill." She covered her face. "Oh, what a mess I've made of things."

A male voice called Tamzin's name.

Tamzin jumped to her feet. "That's Roger. I'll see what he wants, and I'll be right back."

"Do you believe her?" Aunt Jinny asked in a low voice after Tamzin left the room.

"Yes, but she's certainly gone to a lot of trouble to indulge her granddaughter," Harriet said with disapproval in her voice.

Aunt Jinny chuckled. "As an indulgent grandmother myself, I know how badly she must have wanted to please Pip. I want to spoil Sebastian and Sophie every chance I get. It's a grandparent's privilege."

"Regardless, she needs to return Petey at once."

"Agreed." Aunt Jinny said.

Tamzin reappeared and resumed her seat. "I don't want my husband to know what I've done. I'm hoping I can count on your discretion. Now, what should I do?"

"Return Petey first thing in the morning," Harriet told her without hesitation.

Tamzin nodded. "I'll drive over to Whitby bright and early and bring him back. I promise." Ducking her head, she added in a meek voice, "I feel so ashamed. Do you think Gwen will ever forgive me?"

"I don't know," Harriet said. "She's been very upset, unable to sleep or eat properly."

"I think she'll be so thankful to have Petey back that she'll be willing to overlook your crime," Aunt Jinny said.

The word *crime* brought Tamzin up short. "Crime? Does that mean you want to press charges?"

"That's not our place to decide," Harriet said. "Gwen might want to, and, ultimately, it's up to her."

"If Lady has puppies, it's only right and fair that Gwen have the pick of the litter. Do you think she would like that? Do you think that will help her to forgive me?"

Harriet rose from the armchair. There was no need to drag their conversation out any further. "I don't know how Gwen will react to your offer. You'll have to settle that between the two of you."

Aunt Jinny rose as well, slinging her shoulder bag over one arm. "We're counting on you to keep your word, Tamzin. Fetch the dog first thing in the morning and return him to his rightful owner."

"I will, I promise." Tamzin stood up, shoulders stooped and an expression of humiliation on her face. "I'll have Roger open the store and take care of business until I've delivered Petey safely to Gwen. Poor Pip will miss him terribly."

"Not nearly as much as Gwen has missed him," Harriet said. "After all, Pip will still have Lady. And she can watch Petey when the competition is televised."

Tamzin's expression brightened. "What a wonderful idea!" Then she ducked her head. "I hate to ask, Harriet—you've already been kinder than I deserve by not calling in the detective constable— but could I trouble you to come with me in the morning when I return the dog to Gwen? I can call you as soon as I get back to the village with him."

Harriet felt a stirring of compassion for the woman. "Yes, I'll go with you. If for no other reason than to see the delight on Gwen's face when she sees Petey."

"But what will I say to her?" Tamzin asked "How can I ever explain so she'll understand?"

Aunt Jinny provided the answer, repeating what Will had told them earlier. "Honesty is the best policy."

With that, they said their goodbyes.

As Harriet settled into the front seat of her aunt's vehicle, she reached into her purse to retrieve her cell phone.

"Who are you calling?" Aunt Jinny asked, starting the ignition.

"I'm calling Gwen," Harriet replied with a broad grin. "I want to tell her that Petey is coming home tomorrow. I daresay she'll have the first good night's sleep she's had in two weeks."

Her aunt chuckled. "Or she'll be so excited that she won't sleep a wink."

CHAPTER TWENTY-THREE

The next morning when Polly arrived at the clinic, Harriet greeted her with a bright smile and a steaming cup of coffee. She'd felt blissfully lighthearted ever since she'd called Gwen the night before to tell her, without going into detail, that Petey was safe and sound and would be returned to her first thing in the morning. The woman's exclamations of delight had filled Harriet's heart with joy.

"Brace yourself, Polly. I've got good news. We found Petey. I'm going to make sure he gets home safely this morning."

Polly opened her mouth and shut it again. The astonishment on her face quickly changed to joy and relief. "That's wonderful!" Totally ignoring the cup of coffee in her hands, she bombarded Harriet with questions. "He's okay, right? Where was he? How did you find him? Who took him in the first place?"

Harriet laughed. "It wasn't a tall man at all. It was a tall *woman*. Tamzin Pickers."

"Tamzin?" Polly exclaimed. "But why would she do such a horrible thing?"

"Can't talk about it now," Harriet said, slipping on her corduroy jacket. She'd seen Tamzin's vehicle pull up out front. True to her word, the woman must have fetched Petey at the crack of dawn.

Though Polly voiced a protest, Harriet dashed out the door, calling over her shoulder, "I promise to tell you everything when I get back."

"Don't forget you've got two puppies to vaccinate this afternoon," Polly called after her.

Harriet raised a hand in acknowledgment. She had no intention of staying at Gwen's any longer than necessary. She just wanted to make sure her friend's reunion with her beloved dog went smoothly. And she wanted to make sure that Tamzin gave a full explanation of her outrageous behavior. Then she could return to the clinic with her mind less burdened than it had been for some time.

Greeting Tamzin with a cheery, "Good morning," Harriet slid into the passenger seat. Before buckling her seat belt, she turned to peer over the seat at Petey. The dog peeped through the door of the doggie carrier with bright eyes. "Hey, Petey, how's our good boy?" Harriet crooned.

The dog, recognizing a familiar voice, wagged his tail. Harriet could hear it thumping against the walls of the plastic carrier. To Tamzin, she said, "I hope you didn't have any trouble convincing your granddaughter to allow you to take Petey away."

"Not at all," Tamzin assured her as she drove out of the parking lot. "I told her I felt confident that Lady would have a litter of puppies in two months or so. In the meantime, we'll watch Petey perform at the London dog show on the telly. We're making a special occasion out of the event with fish and chips, ice cream, and sticky toffee pudding."

"That's a great idea," Harriet said.

They rode in silence for most of the short time it took to get from Harriet's to Gwen's. At one point, Harriet gave Tamzin a sidelong glance. The woman had dressed with care, probably trying to boost her morale—or her courage. Not a hair was out of place. Her makeup was perfectly applied, and she smelled pleasantly of roses.

"I feel awful about what I've done," Tamzin finally said. "I must have been daft for the past couple of weeks." She shook her head, obviously embarrassed. "I really do hope Gwen can forgive me."

"My grandfather used to say 'all's well that ends well,'" Harriet said, smiling at her. "This is a happy ending. Petey is coming home none the worse for wear, and I think Gwen is a kindhearted woman who will forgive you, considering the circumstances. She doesn't have children or grandchildren of her own, but I think she'd do anything for them if she did."

"I want you all to know that my daughter took great care of the dog. The best food, all his favorite treats, and even a new bed to sleep in. We spared no expense."

Harriet murmured, "That was good of you."

Tamzin added in a sheepish tone, "My daughter and her husband don't know the details. They think I paid a stud fee. If Gwen is truly angry, I'll get the money to her. Somehow. And like I said, if Lady does have a litter, perhaps Gwen would like a puppy. I can promise her the pick of the litter." She regarded Harriet anxiously. "Do you think she'd like that? I know I've already asked you that, but what do you think?"

All Harriet could say was, "We'll see." She had no idea how Gwen would react when she learned the truth. At the moment, Harriet was more concerned with giving Petey a physical examination to reassure herself that he was ready and able to perform in the upcoming competition. But there would be time for that after his reunion with Gwen.

Soon, she and Tamzin walked up the narrow sidewalk to Gwen's residence. Harriet carried Petey while Tamzin led the way, a resigned expression on her face and a reluctant slump to her shoulders.

"I feel so ashamed," she said as she stepped up with Harriet to the front door.

"I know you do, but you're taking the first step toward righting this wrong," Harriet replied. Her heart raced with excitement. As a vet, she often had to do painful things. Reuniting Petey to his rightful owner was something she really looked forward to. Finding a home for Smoky had been a joy too.

Before Tamzin could knock on the door, it was yanked open. Gwen must have been watching for them from the front window. She gave a cry of delight when she saw Petey, who began squirming vigorously to get to his owner.

Harriet handed him over with a laugh.

"Oh, Petey, my little Petey!" Gwen clutched her dog to her chest, laughing as he licked her face, his tail wiggling impossibly fast. Despite the dark circles under her eyes from too many sleepless nights, Gwen's cheeks bloomed with color. Her eyes glistened with unshed tears. She led the way to the sitting room and sat on the couch, fussing over Petey.

Harriet watched them with a happy smile. She could hardly wait to tell Van that he could officially call off the hunt. At long last, Petey was home.

"Do sit down," Gwen urged. "I want to hear everything. Where did you find my dear boy?" She cuddled Petey and cooed to him.

Harriet gently nudged Tamzin. She would stay beside the pet store owner for moral support, but Tamzin needed to tell Gwen her story.

Taking her cue, Tamzin cleared her throat. She sat up straight on the edge of the armchair, where she was seated. "I took your dog, Gwen. It was a horrible thing to do. I know that now. I meant no harm. I want you to know that. I'm truly sorry."

Gwen appeared more stunned than angry. "You took Petey? But why?"

"Begin at the beginning—with your granddaughter's accident," Harriet told Tamzin gently.

Tamzin nodded and relayed the story she'd told Harriet and Aunt Jinny the night before. She rushed through it, slightly breathless, her face flushed, as if eager to have this ordeal over and done with. Harriet couldn't blame her.

Gwen listened attentively, wide-eyed.

At one point, Petey jumped from her lap and headed for the kitchen. When he darted down the hall, they could hear the bell on his collar tinkling as he explored one room after the other. Harriet guessed the terrier was making sure his space had not been invaded by strangers—or other dogs. The breed was very territorial. Only when Petey had assured himself that all was well with his world did he return to the sitting room and resume his perch on the sofa next to Gwen.

"So, it was you that Jane Birtwhistle saw that night carrying Petey away?" Gwen asked with a slight frown wrinkling her brow. "It wasn't a tall man at all?"

Tamzin nodded. "I took him. I'm sorry. I don't even know what to say. My behavior was inexcusable. I wanted to make Pip happy, and I knew from talking to you before that I couldn't afford the stud fee. But that's no excuse. I wanted to help Pip take her mind off her injuries, and I know I went too far." With a heavy sigh, she added, "Gwen, what can I do to make amends? I'll find some way to pay the stud fee if that's what it will take for you to know how sorry I am. If Lady has puppies, you can have the pick of the litter too." Her tone was contrite, her expression anxious.

"How did you get Petey out of the house?" Gwen asked.

"He was in the garden," Tamzin explained. "I had a couple of dog treats in my pocket. One sniff, and he was willing to follow me anywhere. It helped that he already knew me. I toweled him off in my car then put him in the dog crate I keep in the back and drove him straight to my daughter's home in Whitby."

A spark of anger lit in Gwen's eyes. "So when Jane and I came into your store and told you that Petey had been kidnapped, you pretended to comfort me, but really you knew exactly what had happened and where Petey was."

Tamzin hung her head. "Yes, but I also knew he was safe."

The spark blazed. "You let us suspect Billy Brindle and Rupert Decker and even Alistair Marling. I've been calling my fellow competitors to see if they know anything. We've disrupted a lot of people's lives because of this."

Tamzin remained silent. What could she say?

Harriet stayed silent rather than rush to Tamzin's defense. She and Gwen would have to work this out on their own.

Then the spark of anger in Gwen's eyes changed to a gleam of curiosity. "Why didn't you say something when we were in the shop? You knew how upset I was. You saw for yourself my anguish, my pain. But you just stood there."

Tamzin's face became a mask of regret. "I can't explain my behavior. I did what I did for Pip. We've all been worried sick about her. I can only plead a case of temporary insanity. Not that that's an excuse for what I've put you through."

"Did you send the note so I wouldn't worry?" Gwen asked.

"I didn't send it. Pip did," Tamzin explained. "I didn't find out until later that she'd done it. You see, I'd explained to her that you'd allowed Petey to come for a brief visit, hoping he and Lady would have puppies. I told her she could write you a thank-you note afterward. Pip jumped the gun. I suppose she wanted you to know that Petey was having a good visit."

Gwen rose, walked over to a small desk, and returned with the letter and the sheet of printer paper with Petey's photo. "Did your granddaughter send the photo too?" She handed the papers to Tamzin, who took them with another sigh.

"I sent the photo," Tamzin confessed. "When I found out that Pip had sent the letter and how she'd worded it, I was afraid you might think Petey was in danger of some sort, so I sent the photo to let you know he was safe and happy."

There was a long, long pause before Harriet realized she was holding her breath. She tried to read Gwen's expression. What was she thinking? She didn't have to wait long to find out.

"Pip must be a very special child," Gwen said, her tone thick with emotion.

"Oh, she is," Tamzin readily agreed. "I know I'm her grandmother and I'm expected to dote on her, which I do, but our kinship aside, she really is the sweetest girl. And she's suffered so much since the accident. It seemed such a little thing to do, to take Petey so her wish for puppies could come true. I truly meant no harm. Please believe me, and tell me how I can make amends."

Harriet sat rigid in her chair. Here it was—the moment of truth. Would Gwen hold a grudge? Would she press charges?

Gwen glanced down at Petey now dozing comfortably in the corner of the couch. Her lips curled up in a smile, and her expression became one of doting fondness. "I know what it's like to love someone to distraction. You have your Pip, and I have my Petey." She straightened and laced her thin fingers together. "Should Lady have puppies, I'd like the pick of the litter."

Harriet let out a relieved sigh.

Tamzin beamed. "Yes, of course, absolutely." Her cheeks flushed with pleasure and relief.

"I forgive you and am willing to let bygones be bygones." Gwen looked at Tamzin. "And I won't press charges," she went on in a firm voice. "But you need to know that the last two weeks have been the worst of my life. I had such nightmares about what might have happened to my little Petey." Gwen shuddered and closed her eyes.

"It was a dreadful thing to put you through," Tamzin acknowledged. "I can't tell you how sorry I am."

"I only wish you'd trusted me enough to come and talk to me about what you wanted. We could have worked out some sort of financial arrangement. After all, I considered you a friend."

"I have no explanation for that," Tamzin said. "That's what I should have done in the first place. Taking Petey without your permission was so foolish. I can't tell you how bad I feel." After taking a deep breath, she added, "I also think it's only right that Petey get a lifetime supply of his favorite chews. Anytime you need them, come into the shop, and they're on the house."

"What a nice gesture," Harriet said approvingly. "I think you should accept, Gwen."

"I said I'd take a puppy," Gwen reminded them.

"Certainly, you'll get pick of the litter if there is one," Tamzin promised. "But please let me do this too. It's the very least I can do, and it's guaranteed, while the litter isn't."

Gwen smiled. "All right then. I accept. And I wonder if you might allow me to write to Pip, to thank her for showing Petey such warm hospitality and taking good care of him."

Harriet smiled at that, and Tamzin's face lit up like a Christmas tree. "She'd love a real letter in the mail," she said. "If you wrote it as though Petey dictated it to you, that would really tickle her."

Harriet added, "Tamzin and Pip are getting together on the night of the competition to watch Petey perform."

Gwen's eyes twinkled. "Seems like several people I know will be watching that evening."

Harriet laughed. "Several? I think the entire village will be watching and cheering Petey on."

Smiling broadly now, Gwen said in a low, confidential tone, "I feel certain he'll take the top prize in his division."

"And then he'll go on to compete for grand champion, right?" Tamzin asked.

Gwen nodded.

Harriet glanced at the sleeping terrier. She hated to disturb him after the upheaval he'd been through the last couple of weeks. She would arrange for Gwen to bring Petey to the clinic later. "I have a hunch Petey will take the top prize."

"One can hope," Gwen replied with a smile.

CHAPTER TWENTY-FOUR

And there you have it." Harriet perched on the edge of Polly's desk as she finished relaying what had happened.

Harriet had called Van while Tamzin drove her back to the clinic. Eager to hear all the details, the detective constable had arrived shortly after she did. Polly had put the kettle on. Both listened wide-eyed as Harriet explained how and why Tamzin had been responsible for Petey's disappearance.

Polly shook her head in clear amazement. "I'd never have guessed it was Tamzin."

Van gave them both a bleak smile. "I never suspected her either. What sort of police officer am I?"

Polly was quick to come to his defense. "But Van, how could you have known? All we had to go on was what Jane Birtwhistle told us—a tall man in yellow rain gear. None of us thought to suspect a woman."

"Harriet did."

"Not right away, and it was a lucky guess more than anything else," Harriet said. "It wasn't until I saw the photo of Petey gnawing on that chew and Gwen said it was his favorite kind. Who else would have known that but the person who'd sold the treats to Gwen in the first place? But it was just as likely that the kidnapper had stumbled across the treat by a stroke of luck and Tamzin had nothing to do with it. Talking to her was really a long shot, and it's lucky she confessed when we confronted her."

"Is Gwen going to press charges? Tamzin is guilty of stealing her property. Do you think I should let Gwen know what her options are under the law?" Van ran a hand through his hair.

"You'll likely want to follow up with Gwen about the situation so you can officially close the case, but I don't think she'll be pressing any charges," Harriet told him. "Gwen has forgiven Tamzin for what she did. They're moving on."

Before Van could pursue the matter further, Harriet's cell phone vibrated in her coat pocket. Doreen Danby's name flashed across the screen. "One second. I need to take this," Harriet said, swiping to answer the call.

"Are you busy? Can you get away?" her friend asked without prelude.

"I'm free until this afternoon. What's up?"

"I'd like you to meet me in the cemetery and show me Bradley Welks's grave," Doreen said in a tone edged with excitement.

"I'm happy to do that, but wouldn't it be more appropriate for Will to show you?" Harriet asked.

"He's making hospital visits," Doreen explained. "I'd really like to get some photographs of the grave while there's still some decent daylight left. I don't have long because we're due for a storm, and the dark clouds are already rolling in. Tom is working on this wonderful project. I'll tell you all about it when we meet up."

"I'll be right there." Harriet's heart felt lighter than it had in days as she ended the call. Petey was safely home. Gwen would go to

London as planned. And Tom and Doreen were discovering the bonds in their extended family. All was right with the world.

"Polly, I'm headed over to the church to meet up with Doreen Danby. There's nothing else on the schedule until those vaccinations this afternoon, right?"

"Actually, the client had to cancel and has rescheduled for next week, so you're free for the rest of the day."

"Great. I'm sure I won't be too long. Just call me if I'm needed anywhere." Turning to Van, Harriet added, "Thanks again for all your help."

She retrieved her purse from a file cabinet in the surgery, slipping her cell phone in the outside pocket. As she dashed out the door, she donned a jacket. The temperature had dropped, and those dark clouds Doreen had mentioned were indeed rolling in from the sea. She hoped her friend wouldn't want to linger too long in the cemetery, or they'd both be chilled to the bone. They were likely to get soaked to the skin as well.

Doreen was already at the church when Harriet arrived. She had bundled up in a thick flannel jacket and wore a red wool cap pulled down over her ears. She clutched a small digital camera in one hand and a slender ceramic vase of chrysanthemums in the other. "Thanks for coming, especially on such short notice. I really wanted to get this done for Tom while we've still got some sunlight." She glanced at the sky.

Harriet followed her gaze. From somewhere nearby she could hear the faint buzzing of some kind of machinery. A saw perhaps? "Those are lovely flowers. Why do you need a photo of the grave?"

Doreen fell into step beside her. "Tom is putting together an online scrapbook, scanning in photos and those copies of the church records. He's even scanned the photo of Rip from the old newspaper. He wants to make the album available to the whole family. He's leaving space for comments so the cousins can add their thoughts and memories about Malcolm and Bradley and World War II. It'll be a great opportunity to learn about them."

"What a wonderful idea!" Harriet exclaimed. "And the flowers?"

"I thought they'd add some color to the photographs," Doreen told her.

The buzzing noise grew louder as she caught a glimpse of Amos Charlton, the sexton, who wielded a large electric trimmer along the eastern edge of the church property. He caught a glimpse of them and nodded. Harriet raised a hand in greeting.

They walked through the damp grass, passing headstones of all shapes and sizes, some leaning heavily to the side as though tipsy. Others stood straight and tall like dutiful sentries. The grounds were well cared for, Harriet noted. Mr. Charlton took his job seriously, keeping everything tidy.

"Some of the cousins who haven't been in touch with one another in years are now chatting again on the phone and exchanging emails," Doreen continued. "Tom even set up a conference call with a couple of them the other night."

Harriet pointed. "There it is. Bradley Welks."

Doreen moved toward the modest headstone. After a pause to read the engraving, she bent down to set the vase of flowers beside the marker. She stepped away to survey her handiwork then shifted the vase and sighted the result through her camera lens. "That's better. I want to be able to get all the words in the photo."

Harriet nodded, staying well back to make sure she wasn't obstructing Doreen's view.

As Doreen took several shots, some from a distance and others close up, Mr. Charlton came to join them. He removed his cap. "Found a kinsman, did you? Would you ladies like me to take a few snaps of the two of you in front of his grave?"

"Thank you for the offer, Mr. Charlton. I'm not related to the man buried here, but Doreen's husband is," Harriet said.

"We believe he's a great-uncle of my husband, Tom Danby." Doreen smiled.

The man smiled back. He had the bushiest eyebrows Harriet had ever seen. "Nice flowers." He pointed a gnarled finger at the vase. "If you change your mind, I'm happy to oblige." He plopped his cap on his head.

"On second thought," Doreen began, "I would appreciate you taking a picture for us." She turned to Harriet. "I'd like a picture with both of us in front of Bradley's grave. After all, we wouldn't be here without you caring enough to investigate."

Harriet dutifully went to stand beside Doreen, who showed Mr. Charlton the viewfinder and told him which button to push. He snapped a few pictures.

"Now just you, Doreen," Harriet urged. "It'll be nice to have one with you next to the grave. The cousins will enjoy that."

She stepped away again, and Mr. Charlton snapped a few shots and then held the camera out to Doreen. "There you go, Mrs. Danby."

"Brilliant," Doreen said, beaming. "I think these will go on the same page as the photo of Rip, along with the ones Tom took of the dog collar and medal."

When Mr. Charlton gave them a puzzled frown, Harriet explained about Doreen's family album project. His frown deepened. "You say you took snaps of a dog collar and some sort of war medal?"

Doreen nodded. "They turned up in the community lost and found at the police station. Detective Constable Worthington brought them to Harriet's attention. It turns out that the man who's buried in this grave owned the dog. His name was Bradley Welks, and he's my husband's great-uncle, like I said. It's a bit of a mystery where the items came from, but we're enjoying the process of digging into it."

"I reckon I know who put them in the lost and found at the station," Mr. Charlton said. "It was me." He stabbed a gnarled thumb toward his chest.

Harriet's mouth fell open as scrambled thoughts began to fall into place. She recalled seeing the freshly dug flower bed along the south wall of the church. "The daffodils?"

Doreen stared at her in abject confusion.

Mr. Charlton's eyes twinkled with humor. "That's right. I planted them along that wall." He pointed. "Pastor Will is right fond of daffodils. When I turned over the dirt, I found those things—the old dog collar and some sort of medallion. Something from the war, it looked like. I almost threw them in the rubbish bin but then decided not to. Someone might want them."

"It was a medal awarded to a search and rescue dog for gallantry," Doreen explained. "A Dickin Medal from World War II."

"You don't say." The sexton appeared astonished and pleased at the same time.

"It's true," Doreen told him.

"And it's a long story. Too long to tell with those clouds rolling in," Harriet said. "But you've solved the final piece of the puzzle for us. We couldn't figure out how the artifacts got to the police station. Now we know."

"We still haven't learned how they ended up buried here on the church grounds though," Doreen pointed out.

"I reckon someone buried the old dog there along the wall a long time ago. I found a scrap of material. Might have been a bit of flannel from an old blanket maybe. They probably put him there so he could stay close to his master."

"So now you're a part of the story, Mr. Charlton," Harriet said. "I think you should stand next to the headstone with Doreen, and I'll take a photo of the two of you for the album."

Mr. Charlton hesitated, but Doreen eagerly took him by the arm. They stood on either side of the headstone while Harriet snapped a couple of photos.

"You say the *dog* won the medal, and not the man who owned the dog?" Mr. Charlton repeated.

"That's right. But it's too cold out here to tell the tale," Doreen said. "Let's go into the church and ask Claire to give us a cup of tea. Then I'll tell you all about it."

CHAPTER TWENTY-FIVE

Mr. Charlton's newly planted daffodil bed and Rip's Dickin Medal for gallantry were the hot topics of conversation at Aunt Jinny's cottage when friends and family gathered to watch the London dog show on television.

Harriet, feeling a flutter of excitement, arrived early to help her aunt set up the refreshment table. The previous weeks had been stressful. For the first time in several days, she'd been aware of the tension leaving her neck and shoulders. She had slept soundly too for several nights without being haunted by Petey's disappearance, and the change was refreshing.

"I've been so looking forward to watching the competition," she said as she bustled around her aunt's kitchen looking for a large bowl to fill with snacks. The tantalizing aroma of spiced apple cider warming on the stove wafted through the room, along with that of a large steak and kidney pie straight from the oven. Harriet took a deep, appreciative sniff. "I feel as giddy as a little kid on Christmas morning."

Aunt Jinny laughed. "I'm feeling rather festive myself. And a bit jittery too. I can only imagine how Gwen Higginbottom must be feeling right now. Do you think Petey gets nervous before a competition?"

"That little scamp?" Harriet chuckled. "I think Petey's a bit of a show-off. He's enjoying the attention, I'm sure. I don't think he gets nervous, but I'm sure he's excited. He's bound to respond to all the hullabaloo and Gwen's mood as well."

Soon Polly and Van arrived with soft drinks and plastic cups. "Tonight's the night," Polly exclaimed. "I know Petey's going to win the grand championship."

Harriet gave her a hug. "I hope you're right."

"I hate to think of all the disappointed villagers if he doesn't," Van added.

Aunt Jinny's son, Anthony, arrived with his wife, Olivia, and their six-year-old twins, Sebastian and Sophie.

"Where should I put this?" Olivia asked her mother-in-law, hefting a large tray with assorted cheeses and cold meats.

"Don't forget, there's a pan of sticky toffee pudding in the boot," Anthony reminded her.

"I'll get that," Harriet offered. She'd developed quite a fondness for Olivia's sticky toffee pudding. "Want to help me?" she asked the twins.

The three of them darted outside. It had turned cold and drizzly again, but Harriet didn't mind. The excitement of watching the highly anticipated televised competition with friends and family made her feel warm all over. She had just removed the pudding dish from the boot of Anthony's car when the Danbys pulled up. Sebastian and Sophie bounced up and down, eager to play with the Danby youngsters who tumbled out of the family vehicle—all legs and arms and broad smiles.

"Something smells delicious. What is it?" Harriet asked as Tom walked toward her with a large slow cooker.

"Chicken curry. An old family recipe," Doreen answered for him.

"From a great-great-uncle who served with the British Army in India back in the day," Tom added.

"I brought a bilberry pie too." Doreen held up a covered pie plate. "I know you're rather fond of it."

"I can't wait," Harriet told her, leading the way to Aunt Jinny's cottage. She was now hungrier than ever.

While the children played in a corner of the living room, the adults clustered around the refreshment table, discussing Rip's long-lost medal and Petey's chances of winning the grand championship. When Will arrived a short while later, bearing a large pizza box, everyone was already eating and drinking. Doreen was sharing the saga of Bradley Welks and his gallant dog with Anthony and Olivia.

"And to think, the old dog collar and the medallion were found in the daffodil bed at the church," Doreen declared.

Everyone listened as Tom explained how he was putting together an online album detailing Bradley's service as an air raid warden in London. When Harriet slipped away to the kitchen, Will followed.

"Can I help?" he asked.

She smiled, handing him a package of rolls to open.

"Gwen called before she left for London," he told her.

Harriet's eyebrows shot up. She felt a tingle of apprehension. "Is everything okay?

Will nodded. "She wanted me to pray for safe travels for her and Petey."

"I've been praying for them too," Harriet said. "But my prayers have been rather selfish, I'm afraid. I really want Petey to win the grand championship cup. After all Gwen has been through, it seems a suitable reward for her suffering and for her easy forgiveness toward Tamzin."

"So, it's not enough for you that he wins in his category or division?" Will quirked an eyebrow.

"I feel certain he'll do that. But I want him to bring home the big trophy. It would be such a blessing for Gwen and would make up for all the stress and anxiety she's gone through in the last couple of weeks."

Her prediction proved right when a short twenty minutes later, Lord Peter Wimsey did indeed win first prize in the terrier category. Everyone clapped, and the youngsters whooped with joy.

"Did he win? Did he win?" Sophie asked, bouncing up and down in her seat.

Aunt Jinny scooped up her little granddaughter. "Petey won this round of the contest. Now we have to wait for the grand finale."

"Petey looks quite dapper in his new plaid collar, compliments of Tamzin Pickers, I was told," Will said.

"That's the Robertson tartan," Polly observed. "I wonder if it's personal to Gwen in some way. Clan plaid, maybe. Think the judges will take note of that?"

"Should they?" Tom asked, spooning up some of Doreen's excellent curry. "Gwen's maiden name was Robertson. Her father used to tell us village boys some very exciting stories of his ancestors and their battles." He chuckled. "Looking back on it, I'm pretty sure he embellished the facts to put us on the edge of our seats."

Harriet peered closely at the television, studying the dog's plaid dog collar. She couldn't tell the difference between one clan's tartan and another. They all seemed to be a variation on a theme—either red and green or blue and green. She supposed those in the know could distinguish one from another. Maybe one day she'd be able to do the same.

Aunt Jinny took advantage of a station break to encourage everyone to help themselves to more food. The youngsters gobbled up the cocktail franks on toothpicks with plaid frills, which Aunt Jinny had dubbed "Petey franks" for the occasion.

Harriet sidled up to Will a short while later as he enjoyed a helping of steak and kidney pie. "By the way," she said in low voice, "we're not mentioning Tamzin's role in all the mischief. It would be too embarrassing and serves no good purpose at all. We'd rather not risk damaging her business over a lapse in judgment in her personal life."

"I think that's wise." Will glanced around the dining room where everyone lingered near the refreshment table. "Some here already know what happened, right?"

"Yes, but Polly, Van, and Aunt Jinny can be trusted to be discreet."

Will snapped his fingers. "Oh, that reminds me. I ran into an acquaintance of yours the other day. I gave him a lift, and we had a pleasant though brief conversation."

"An acquaintance of mine?" Harriet couldn't imagine who he was referring to.

"Young Clarence Decker," Will said.

"Really? How did that come about?"

"I was returning from a home visit when I saw him kneeling on the side of the road," Will told her. "It looked like he was lifting something out of the grass. I stopped and saw it was an injured pheasant with a broken wing. Hit by a car, Clarence presumed. I offered him a lift and stowed his bicycle. He certainly couldn't pedal his way home with a wounded bird in his arms."

"That was kind of you." Harriet was gratified that the teenager had such a tender heart for animals. She thought again of maybe hiring him to help out at the clinic now and then. He might enjoy riding along occasionally when she was called to assist with the delivery of a calf, or when it was time to trim Dipsy Doodle's hooves again.

Will flushed. "Kindness is one of the fruits of the Spirit, as you'll recall. And I believe that good deeds like the kind Clarence does should be encouraged. How better to do that than to provide active support?"

Before they could continue with their conversation, Van called out that the winning dogs in each category were being examined by the judges in the final round. Everyone crowded closer to the television. Harriet felt an uptick in her pulse when she caught sight of Gwen and Petey making their way around the ring. Gwen appeared calm and professional in a dark blue skirt suit and sensible shoes. Petey appeared to be smiling—yes, smiling—as though he had the prize in the bag.

"He's full of sauce," Polly said. "Look at him." With a wink at Harriet, she began chanting, "Petey, Petey, Petey."

The children joined in, giggling. So did Harriet. Even long and lanky sixteen-year-old Thommy lost some of his teenage self-consciousness to chant along with the others.

After the canine contestants promenaded around the ring, a judge examined them for physical flaws, studying their teeth, eyes, and legs. The judge patted one and peered closely at another, prodding the dog's hips.

Harriet's heart pounded. She tried hard not to hold her breath in anticipation. Polly took her hand and squeezed it.

When Harriet thought about Tamzin Pickers over in Whitby at this very moment watching the same program with her granddaughter, she sent up a silent prayer that the little girl would adjust to life in a wheelchair. Was it all right to pray that Lady would soon have a litter of puppies? She hoped the Lord wouldn't consider that a frivolous request.

They all fell silent as the main judge strode to the podium to make the final announcement. "Ladies and gentlemen," she said, "the judges have made their decisions. Every single one of the entries this year are excellent representatives of their breeds, but there can only be one Best in Show. And now, without any further ado, the second runner-up is…Kasey of Skunk Hollow, owner Martha Kintner."

A petite woman holding the leash of an enormous Great Dane beamed and walked forward to take her place beside the judge. Harriet marveled again at the sheer size of the majestic dog.

The judge took a deep breath. "The first runner-up is…" Harriet didn't know whether she wanted to hear Petey's name or not. Not hearing it meant there was still a chance he could be the grand champion. Then the man said, "Kingsford's Golden Harley, owner, Isaac Kramer."

Harriet had known from the moment she'd seen the exuberant, cheerful golden retriever that he was the perfect specimen of his breed. Confident, playful, noble—she'd felt Harley was the one to beat. So now, maybe…

Finally, after what seemed like an eternity, the judge said, "And now, what we've all been waiting for. Ladies, and gentlemen, the Best in Show prize goes to…"

The room was so quiet, Harriet thought the others must have stopped breathing. She wondered if everyone's heart was beating as hard as hers was. She felt ready to jump out of her skin.

Finally, the judge took another deep breath and announced, "Lord Peter Whimsey, owner, Gwen Higginbottom!"

The audience at Aunt Jinny's house exploded into a cacophony of squealing, clapping, and cheering, and to her own chagrin, Harriet burst into tears. "Happy tears," she assured little Sophie, who had stopped jumping up and down to peer at Harriet's wet cheeks with concern.

Aunt Jinny hurried to the kitchen to retrieve several bottles of chilled sparkling grape juice. "I bought these hoping we'd be toasting Petey's victory," she explained. "And here we are."

More cheering and clapping followed when Tom announced that he and Doreen planned to throw a victory party at their home for Petey and Gwen. "And we want to introduce everyone to Rip too—virtually, of course. We want to share his story."

As everyone began to ask how they might help, Harriet took Doreen by the elbow and pulled her to one side. "I wonder if I could ask a favor," she said softly.

Doreen beamed. "Name it, neighbor."

"Would you be willing to invite Rupert and Clarence Decker to the festivities?"

Arching an eyebrow, Doreen asked, "Seriously?"

"Seriously. I've been thinking about one of Will's recent sermons, about Jesus's parable of the great banquet, where His followers were encouraged to invite the poor, the crippled, the lame, and the blind. I realize the Deckers aren't poor or crippled, but they are outsiders. I don't know if they'll even come, but it would be a nice gesture to invite them anyway. Don't you think so?"

Doreen pursed her lips. Finally, she nodded. "I'll invite them."

Harriet gave her friend a hearty hug. "Thank you. You won't be sorry."

"I certainly hope not. If young Clarence arrives with a little owl in his pocket, he'll be the hit of the party."

"One taste of your cooking, and Rupert will be all smiles," Harriet said with a chuckle.

"You know, that's something I'd like to see—Rupert Decker smiling. Just imagining it makes me happy." She wandered off to talk to Aunt Jinny.

Will took Doreen's place by Harriet's side. "I suppose we couldn't ask for more of a perfect ending," he said.

Harriet took a sip of sparking juice. "It's *almost* a perfect ending."

"Oh? What's missing, may I ask?" Will leaned his hip against the table and crossed his arms.

Harriet beamed at him. "Everything will be perfect, simply perfect, when we discover that Petey has successfully sired puppies and Gwen Higginbottom gets to choose the pick of the litter."

She reached out and touched Will's arm. "A lot of the credit goes to you, Will. Your advice about how to approach Tamzin was spot-on. I was ready to go in guns blazing, and you helped me see that the truth, spoken in love, was the best way to go."

Will's eyes softened. "You need to give yourself more credit, Harriet. I think you would have handled it just right without my help. White Church Bay is beginning to trust and respect the new Yankee vet."

Harriet smiled. "Thank you, Will. With every day that goes by, I'm more and more convinced that this 'Yankee vet' is right where she's meant to be."

And that was the honest truth.

FROM THE AUTHOR

Dear Reader,

I hope you have enjoyed this new adventure in Yorkshire with Harriet, Polly, Aunt Jinny, and the other residents of White Church Bay. Many years ago, I visited West Yorkshire and thoroughly enjoyed my time there. There's so much to do, like visiting the Brontë Parsonage Museum in Haworth and taking a ride on one of the heritage railroads, which reminded me of *The Railway Children* by Edith Nesbit, a book I read as a child.

Everything was so picturesque, especially the old churches and cemeteries. As I sat in the St. Michael and All Angels Church where Patrick Brontë was the vicar for over forty years, I tried to imagine what it was like to attend services there with the Brontë sisters. My friend Debbie and I strolled the moors, admiring the sheep and breathing in the brisk summer air. I quite enjoyed everything I ate while in England and quickly developed a fondness for rich, clotted cream on warm scones topped with damson plum jam.

And don't you just want to give Petey a hug? I've owned two Scottish terriers in the past—or maybe I should say they owned me. Hands down, they were the best dogs I ever loved. I miss them still.

Cartoonist Charles Schulz once said, "Happiness is a warm puppy." I wholeheartedly agree!

With joy,
Shirley Raye

ABOUT THE AUTHOR

Shirley Raye Redmond has received numerous awards for both her women's fiction and children's books. Her devotions have appeared in multiple volumes of Guideposts' *All God's Creatures* and *Daily Guideposts,* and she has enjoyed writing several mysteries for Guideposts' Savannah Secrets and Secrets from Grandma's Attic series. Shirley Raye has been married for fifty years to her college sweetheart. They live in the scenic mountains of northern New Mexico near their two children and five grandchildren.

TRUTH BEHIND THE FICTION

If you're as intrigued by World War II history as I am, you may be wondering: Is there such a thing as the Dickin Medal for heroic animals? There is! The story of Rip is a true one. He did indeed receive a medal in 1945 because of his heroic efforts during the London Blitz. The information regarding the recipients of the prestigious award that Harriet discovers on the PDSA website are true. I did, however, tweak a few facts for the sake of my novel. Bradley Welks is a fictional character. The real canine hero was "adopted" by an air raid warden named Mr. E. King. The Dicken Medal that Rip was awarded was sold at auction in 2009 for over thirty-one thousand dollars. Rip is buried in a special PDSA cemetery in Ilford, Essex—along with several other heroic animals who earned the Dickin Medal.

YORKSHIRE YUMMIES

Aunt Jinny's Applesauce Muffins

Who doesn't love a fresh muffin warm from the oven? Here's a recipe for applesauce muffins like the ones Aunt Jinny served to Harriet at the beginning of the story.

Ingredients:

3 cups flour

Pinch of salt

1 teaspoon nutmeg

4 teaspoons baking powder

1 cup sugar

⅔ cup shortening

2 beaten eggs

1 cup apple, peeled and chopped

¼ cup applesauce (any variety)

1 cup milk

1 cup cinnamon sugar

Directions:

1. Mix together flour, salt, nutmeg, baking powder, and sugar.
2. Cut in shortening.
3. Add eggs, apple, applesauce, and milk.
4. Mix until moistened. Pour into greased or lined muffin tins.
5. Bake at 350 degrees for 20 to 25 minutes.
6. Remove from pan while hot.
7. Dip tops of muffins into melted butter and then into cinnamon sugar.

These are best eaten warm, but they're truly yummy anytime!

A Little Bird
Told Me

BY LAURA BRADFORD

Sinking down onto the edge of the closest waiting room chair, Harriet Bailey released a long sigh of relief. "As good as today was, I'll be mighty glad to shut off the lights the moment you head out to your car."

"I'll be rather chuffed, myself." Polly Thatcher tossed her phone into her tote bag, tugged its strap up her arm, and pushed her desk drawer shut. "But today really was fantastic, wasn't it? A new patient, two boarders scheduled for next week, a successful surgery, and you don't have a single new scratch on you anywhere."

Harriet's answering laugh trailed away as a familiar squeaking sound drew near. A longhaired dachshund scurried into view, thanks to the wheeled prosthesis that had given him a new lease on life. "Tonight's the night, Maxwell. You, me, and a can of oil."

"Must you?" Polly asked, resting her hand on the doorknob. "I've grown rather fond of his squeaking."

Harriet reached down, ran her hand along the dog's back, and then returned it to the top of his head for a much-appreciated scratch behind the ears. "I must. Right, Maxwell?"

At Maxwell's answering lick of her hand, she looked up at her receptionist and best friend in the open doorway. "I imagine your plans for this evening are a bit more exciting than mine."

"That remains to be seen."

"But you have a date with a certain bloke we both know, correct?"

Polly's laugh filled the veterinary reception area. "Look at you, using the word *bloke*. Correctly, even."

"And it sounded natural, right?"

Polly pursed her lips as if weighing Harriet's question. "You're getting there."

"I'll take that." Harriet stood and stretched her back. "Give me another six months, and no one will have any inkling I'm not from White Church Bay."

"They'd have to be daft to believe that," Polly teased.

"Good evening, ladies." An attractive thirtysomething man stood in the open door, hands resting on a well-used tool belt. His name, Mike Dane, was scrawled across the belt in thick black ink.

"Good evening, Mike. Heading home?" Harriet asked.

Her temporary handyman gestured around the grounds of Cobble Hill Farm, which Harriet had inherited from her beloved grandfather. "I was thinking about it, unless there's another task you'd like me to get to before Monday?"

"It's like I told you when I hired you," she assured him. "I'm in no rush on the things I need you to do, with the exception of the gallery's roof." The outbuilding that housed Harold Bailey's studio and gallery had a thatched roof in need of some attention.

Mike nodded. "I took care of that today."

She stared at him. "Already?"

"Yes, ma'am."

"Wow. That was fast." Harriet was impressed. "If you've got your receipts for the materials, I'll write you a check now."

He shook his head. "No worries. We can get to that next week."

"Next week it is," she agreed. "Now, go enjoy your weekend."

He tipped his hat at Harriet and then Polly. "You ladies as well." And then he was gone, his long legs quickly carrying him toward the public path along the North Sea.

"I think he should fix lots of things around here." Polly leaned forward in an effort to extend her viewing window. "*Lots* of things."

It was Harriet's turn to laugh. "Wait. I thought Van was taking up the bulk of your dance card lately."

At the mention of the sweet but somewhat shy detective constable, Polly's cheeks flushed crimson. "Van Worthington was born with two left feet," she protested. "We tried dancing together once. Suffice it to say, I had to come up with a way to get him off the dance floor without hurting his feelings."

"How did you manage that?"

"I feigned thirst and exhaustion."

"And being the gentleman he is, Van immediately ushered you to a seat and got you refreshments." Laughing, Harriet shook her head. "Van has no idea what he's in for with you, does he?"

"He does not."

"Poor bloke," Harriet joked before growing more serious. "Really, though, you two are still enjoying each other's company, right?"

"We are. Very much." Polly headed for her car, calling over her shoulder, "I'll see you tomorrow morning. Have fun de-squeaking Maxwell."

"You know I will." Harriet laughed and shut the door on what had been a successful Friday. Moving to England from Connecticut had been a big change—one she was still adjusting to in many ways. But, day by day, she was seeing more and more reasons why it had been the right change to make.

Like her deepening friendship with Polly and her growing patient list.

Particularly telling was the peace and contentment she felt in quiet moments.

Harriet smiled down at her dog, letting him into the kitchen. There was no beating her commute to and from work, with the clinic attached to her home. "Well, Maxwell, it's time. Time for both of us to eat, time for you to get your wheels de-squeaked, and time for me to finally start that book I've—"

Her words broke off at a faint but undeniable thump from somewhere above her head, followed by a muted *meow*.

Groaning, she looked back down at Maxwell. "Sorry, buddy. I'll get to you, I promise. But first I need to go upstairs and see what Charlie has gotten herself into."

She took the stairs two at a time to the top and then stopped to listen.

"Charlie," she called. "Curiosity isn't always a wise trait for cats, sweet girl."

The sound of something rolling was followed by a faint jingling, as of a bell.

She made her way toward the attic door she clearly remembered shutting, though it now stood ajar. The clinic cat peered around it at Harriet, a cobweb attached to her ear, which flicked in vain attempts to dislodge it.

"Charlie," Harriet scolded. "How do you keep getting in there?"

The patchy-haired calico sat back on her haunches, worked the cobweb free with her front paw, and then darted past Harriet to the stairs.

"Fine. Keep your secrets," she said. "But know that this door and your ability to open it will be added to Mike's list for next week."

She stepped forward to push the door closed but stopped as she remembered the bell sound. Curious, she nudged the door open and felt around on the wall to her left for the light switch. One day, when everything about work and the house and the grounds was exactly the way she wanted it to be, she'd spend time going through the piles and piles of boxes up here. But until then, they'd have to wait.

A quick glance around the unfinished space yielded the answer she sought. On the floor, not more than a few feet away, she saw a small, red plastic sphere with a gold bell inside. Harriet picked up the toy then smiled at the curious feline face that appeared beside her at the sound. "Couldn't resist a second look, could you, Charlie-girl?"

The latest in a long line of office cats by that name, Charlie remained silent. She gently pressed a paw against Harriet's leg in a clear request for the ball.

"Let's take this downstairs for you and Maxwell to play with after dinner." She was about to leave when her gaze snagged on the exposed end of an electrical cord. Intrigued, she followed the cord to where it disappeared inside a box in the middle of a stack of other boxes. "I bet you thought that was a snake, didn't you, Charlie?"

She crossed to the stack and pulled back the top flap of the box, intending to wrap the cord up and tuck it inside.

She changed her mind at the sight of the cord's accompanying cassette player and a pile of tapes bearing her grandfather's handwriting.

"What on earth?" she murmured, earning herself a soft meow in response.

She picked up the first cassette and read the label out loud. "'Artie'?" Her thoughts immediately traveled to her grandfather's gallery and the painting he'd done of a duck that garnered giggles from youngsters on a daily basis.

She flipped the tape over, found no additional information, and then reached for the next one in the pile. Across the label, her grandfather had written, MELODY. Again, her thoughts traveled to the gallery and another popular painting, this one of a songbird once owned by fellow White Church Bay resident Meredith Bennett.

Harriet thumbed through the rest of the tapes, the names matching those of animals her grandfather had painted. In fact, she thought nearly every animal that had served as a subject for her grandfather's talent was represented with a tape. At least all the ones she'd seen in his gallery. She supposed there were other paintings that he'd given away and that she'd never seen.

The last one in the pile, however, didn't bear the name of an animal. On that one, her grandfather's writing read, MY STORY.

A nudge on her ankle pulled her attention to the floor. The cat was clearly trying to get a point across. "Okay, Charlie. I know it's dinnertime and you want this toy."

She set the tapes back in the box then picked up the whole thing and carried it out of the attic and down the stairs, Charlie traipsing ahead of her.

When she reached the kitchen, she set the box on the floor next to the table, fed the dog and the cat, heated up some soup, and sat down with the box.

She plugged in the cassette player, praying it still worked. Then she took out the tape labeled MY STORY.

She inserted the tape into the machine and pressed play. Her beloved grandfather's voice filled the room.

"My dear wife, Helen, was a questioner. Didn't matter whether she knew you for years or just met you at the market. She said asking questions and listening to the answers was how families grew closer and strangers became friends. She asked me to make this tape, insisting that someday someone would want my story too, what led me to painting. It's not all that exciting, really, but Helen said it mattered, and I learned early on not to argue with her. So this is for the woman I still feel in my heart every single day."

"Oh, Grandad," Harriet whispered, pressing her hand to her chest. What a gift this tape was.

"I'm not sure whether people realize it, but so many of the animals I've treated over the years have become like family to me. I'm happy to see them when they come in for a checkup, and I worry when they come to me during an illness. Each one has a personality of their own.

Some let me see it the moment I first lay eyes on them. Others make me work for it, revealing various bits and pieces over time."

Harriet found herself nodding. She felt the same way.

"From the timid hamster who prefers to eat when no one is watching to the dog who faithfully cared for a litter of orphaned kittens until they were old enough to thrive on their own, each and every animal that has come through my door has left an indelible impression on my soul. I've often found my words inadequate in describing those impressions. Yet when I put paint to canvas, that changes. Instead of trying to put what I see into words that never seem to do an animal justice, I've found that I can *show* what I see. That, my dear Helen, is the story behind my animal paintings."

A series of squeaks from behind Harriet's chair stole her attention. Parking himself beside her chair, Maxwell leaned against her leg.

"Did you recognize Grandad's voice, boy? He wouldn't have let you squeak at all, would he?" She hit stop on the cassette player. "Let's get your wheels all nice and—"

Her phone rang, cutting her off. After closing time, Polly had the clinic's calls forwarded to Harriet's cell phone. Since she didn't recognize the number, that was clearly what this was, which also meant it was likely an emergency. She answered at once as she hurried back to the clinic in case she needed anything there. "Hello, this is Dr. Harriet Bailey."

A muffled sob came through the phone. "This is Cindy Summerton. I wouldn't be calling at this hour if it wasn't an emergency. I—I don't know what to do."

"Take a deep breath, Cindy. What's wrong?"

"It's my cat, Nessie," the woman wailed. "She always plays outside in the garden while I'm making supper. It's her routine. But when I shook her can of treats to let her know it was time to come inside, she didn't come."

Harriet's stomach twisted at the words, but she got herself under control. Not too long ago, she'd helped reunite a missing show dog with his owner. Surely this wasn't another missing animal so soon. "I'm sure she'll be back, Cindy. She's probably found something interesting to play with."

"No, the gate was open, and it's not supposed to be."

Something caught Harriet's eye. She crossed the room and stared down at her name in block letters across the top of an envelope that had been shoved under the door. "Did you step outside the gate and shake her treats from there?"

"Of course. But there's no sign of her anywhere."

Harriet picked up the envelope and carried it back to Polly's desk, her curiosity sidelined by the needs of the distraught woman in her ear. "I wouldn't panic yet, Cindy. I really—"

"But, Dr. Bailey, I sent Tarquin out to look for her, and he can't find her either."

Harriet started Polly's computer then pulled up the cat's record. She scrolled until she found the information she wanted. "As I suspected, Nessie is chipped."

"Chipped?" Cindy echoed. "What does that mean?"

"Microchipped. If she's turned in to any shelter or vet office, she'll be scanned and traced back to us here."

"I—I guess that's encouraging."

"It is," Harriet said. "But I suspect Nessie will be sitting outside your garden door first thing tomorrow morning. She'll be hungry and tired from her adventure, but every bit as glad to be home as you will be to have her there."

"And if she's not?"

"We'll cross that bridge if we come to it. But Nessie knows she has it good with you, so I'm confident she'll be back." Harriet closed out of Nessie's record and powered off the computer, hoping Cindy couldn't hear that Harriet was trying to convince herself too. But she couldn't ignore the misgivings growing in her mind. "Now get some rest. When Nessie returns, she'll be in need of lots of cuddles from you, your husband, and your beautiful baby boy. Doctor's orders."

Cindy took a deep breath, sounding calmer. "Thank you, Dr. Bailey."

"Of course. Nessie held a very special place in Grandad's heart, as you well know, along with everyone who's ever stepped inside his gallery and seen his painting of her." Harriet grabbed the envelope. "I'll check with you first thing in the morning. If Nessie's not back by then, we'll send out the cavalry."

"I'd appreciate that," Cindy said, the hitch in her voice lessening. "Good night, Dr. Bailey."

"Good night, Cindy."

Harriet ended the call, opened the envelope, and unfolded the single sheet of paper it contained. Ugly block letters chilled her to the bone.

I HAVE NESSIE.

A NOTE FROM THE EDITORS

We hope you enjoyed another exciting volume in the Mysteries of Cobble Hill Farm series, published by Guideposts. For over seventy-five years, Guideposts, a nonprofit organization, has been driven by a vision of a world filled with hope. We aspire to be the voice of a trusted friend, a friend who makes you feel more hopeful and connected.

By making a purchase from Guideposts, you join our community in touching millions of lives, inspiring them to believe that all things are possible through faith, hope, and prayer. Your continued support allows us to provide uplifting resources to those in need. Whether through our communities, websites, apps, or publications, we inspire our audiences, bring them together, and comfort, uplift, entertain, and guide them. Visit us at guideposts.org to learn more.

We would love to hear from you. Write us at Guideposts, P.O. Box 5815, Harlan, Iowa 51593 or call us at (800) 932-2145. Did you love *Show Stopper*? Leave a review for this product on guideposts.org/shop. Your feedback helps others in our community find relevant products.

Find inspiration, find faith, find Guideposts.

Shop our best sellers and favorites at
guideposts.org/shop

Or scan the QR code to go directly to our Shop

**Loved Mysteries of Cobble Hill Farm? Check out
some other Guideposts mystery series!**

SECRETS FROM GRANDMA'S ATTIC

Life is recorded not only in decades or years, but in events and memories that form the fabric of our being. Follow Tracy Doyle, Amy Allen, and Robin Davisson, the granddaughters of the recently deceased centenarian, Pearl Allen, as they explore the treasures found in the attic of Grandma Pearl's Victorian home, nestled near the banks of the Mississippi in Canton, Missouri. Not only do Pearl's descendants uncover a long-buried mystery at every attic exploration, they also discover their grandmother's legacy of deep, abiding faith, which has shaped and guided their family through the years. These uncovered Secrets from Grandma's Attic reveal stories of faith, redemption, and second chances that capture your heart long after you turn the last page.

History Lost and Found
The Art of Deception
Testament to a Patriot
Buttoned Up
Pearl of Great Price
Hidden Riches

SAVANNAH SECRETS

Welcome to Savannah, Georgia, a picture-perfect Southern city known for its manicured parks, moss-covered oaks, and antebellum architecture. Walk down one of the cobblestone streets, and you'll come upon Magnolia Investigations. It is here where two friends have joined forces to unravel some of Savannah's deepest secrets. Tag along as clues are exposed, red herrings discarded, and thrilling surprises revealed. Find inspiration in the special bond between Meredith Bellefontaine and Julia Foley. Cheer the friends on as they listen to their hearts and rely on their faith to solve each new case that comes their way.

The Hidden Gate
A Fallen Petal
Double Trouble
Whispering Bells
Where Time Stood Still
The Weight of Years
Willful Transgressions
Season's Meetings
Southern Fried Secrets
The Greatest of These
Patterns of Deception

The Waving Girl
Beneath a Dragon Moon
Garden Variety Crimes
Meant for Good
A Bone to Pick
Honeybees & Legacies
True Grits
Sapphire Secret
Jingle Bell Heist
Buried Secrets
A Puzzle of Pearls
Facing the Facts
Resurrecting Trouble
Forever and a Day

MYSTERIES OF MARTHA'S VINEYARD

Priscilla Latham Grant has inherited a lighthouse! So with not much more than a strong will and a sore heart, the recent widow says goodbye to her lifelong Kansas home and heads to the quaint and historic island of Martha's Vineyard, Massachusetts. There, she comes face-to-face with adventures, which include her trusty canine friend, Jake, three delightful cousins she didn't know she had, and Gerald O'Bannon, a handsome Coast Guard captain—plus head-scratching mysteries that crop up with surprising regularity.

A Light in the Darkness
Like a Fish Out of Water
Adrift
Maiden of the Mist
Making Waves
Don't Rock the Boat
A Port in the Storm
Thicker Than Water
Swept Away
Bridge Over Troubled Waters
Smoke on the Water
Shifting Sands
Shark Bait

Seascape in Shadows
Storm Tide
Water Flows Uphill
Catch of the Day
Beyond the Sea
Wider Than an Ocean
Sheeps Passing in the Night
Sail Away Home
Waves of Doubt
Lifeline
Flotsam & Jetsam
Just Over the Horizon

Find more inspiring stories in these best-loved Guideposts fiction series!

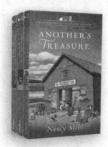

Mysteries of Lancaster County

Follow the Classen sisters as they unravel clues and uncover hidden secrets in Mysteries of Lancaster County. As you get to know these women and their friends, you'll see how God brings each of them together for a fresh start in life.

Secrets of Wayfarers Inn

Retired schoolteachers find themselves owners of an old warehouse-turned-inn that is filled with hidden passages, buried secrets, and stunning surprises that will set them on a course to puzzling mysteries from the Underground Railroad.

Tearoom Mysteries Series

Mix one stately Victorian home, a charming lakeside town in Maine, and two adventurous cousins with a passion for tea and hospitality. Add a large scoop of intriguing mystery, and sprinkle generously with faith, family, and friends, and you have the recipe for *Tearoom Mysteries*.

Ordinary Women of the Bible

Richly imagined stories—based on facts from the Bible—have all the plot twists and suspense of a great mystery, while bringing you fascinating insights on what it was like to be a woman living in the ancient world.

To learn more about these books, visit Guideposts.org/Shop